T0195015

ERESHKIGAL'S VENGEANCE

RACE FOR A CURE AGAINST A PANDEMIC

Carl T. Seaborn

ERESHKIGAL'S VENGEANCE
RACE FOR A CURE AGAINST A PANDEMIC

iUniverse books may be ordered through booksellers or by contacting:

iUniverse
1663 Liberty Drive
Bloomington, IN 47403
www.iuniverse.com
844-349-9409

ISBN: 978-1-6632-3668-5 (sc)
ISBN: 978-1-6632-3669-2 (e)

Library of Congress Control Number: 2022904366

Print information available on the last page.

iUniverse rev. date: 06/08/2022

CHAPTER 1

R alph's working day in Downtown Boston was over. Feeling upbeat, he left the office of his employer, Booximply, and made his way to the underground parking lot where the lights flashed on automatically. With his key fob, he remotely opened the door to his electric company car, got in, and drove off.

Aerosmith's "Walk This Way" was playing on the radio; he sang along wholeheartedly. Once outside the garage, he squinted at the blazing sunshine on this glorious May day. He flipped down the visor. Without a sound, he edged his way through the bustling city traffic and set course for the green Jamaica Plain neighborhood. He passed a poster for the Wake Up the Earth Festival that would be taking place there over the weekend. The swarms of colorfully clad festival goers descending on this place and making it into a party town made him smile, as this matched his good mood.

He finally reached the tranquil Adelaide Street, parked the car, and went up the steps to the home he'd bought together with his wife, Sarah. It was a typical single-family house on that street: on one level and a basement under a saddle roof, built in 1900s, and fully renovated.

Sarah was already home. He found her in the kitchen and kissed her affectionately.

"How was your day, honey?" she asked.

"Oh, fine," he replied. "Made some real progress. I've sold our appointment-scheduling tool."

"That thing you've been working on the last few weeks?"

"Yep. The Massachusetts employment agency—they bought it."

"The employment agency? That must be a major client."

"You can say that again! They're going to use the tool to schedule appointments between job-seekers and their specialized service providers in the regions."

Ralph placed his briefcase on the floor and lifted Sarah up. It didn't take much effort.

"And what's in it for you, Superman?" Sarah joked.

"Outstripping my annual quarterly target. I'll get one hundred and twenty percent of my bonus."

"Cool!"

"So that tool's our showpiece."

He lowered her down until her feet touched the floor. "And how was your day, Lois Lane?"

"Good too. I helped no less than twelve patients at the physio practice."

"Isn't that exhausting?"

"Sure, but it's awesome seeing people starting to feel better after massages or exercises. They're grateful to me, and that's satisfying."

"Like that patient with the paralyzed leg you recently helped learn to walk again?"

"He sent me flowers again today. His previous bouquet had wilted, and I threw it in the organic trash. That reminds me, could you take out the garbage?"

"Sure, tomorrow's collection day, I see."

Ralph rolled the garbage can to the sidewalk. Olivia, the neighbor, was sitting in a chair on her deck, basking in the last rays of sunshine. He didn't know her exact age, but he guessed she had to be in her eighties. She had a brown, puckered face, long gray hair, piercing eyes, and carefully monitored everything happening on their street.

"Hi, Ralph," she said. "How's things with your wife?"

"Just great, Olivia!"

"Still besotted with each other, eh?"

"Sure, like it ought to be with a young couple, right?"

"Well, be careful. Some folks are jealous of happy people." She then gave Ralph a penetrating stare. That made him feel uneasy.

"What do you mean, Olivia?"

"Yep, if the government could, it'd put a tax on being happy to finance its nasty schemes. It's already taken away my husband, during the Vietnam War."

"I know. I'm really sorry for you."

"Wolves they are, yep. They devour your happiness with their unseen teeth. Young people will have a tough time of it too, you mark my words."

"Don't worry, Olivia; we're on our guard, and we won't be messed around."

Ralph went back inside and shook his head. That old Olivia. She was way too suspicious, but she meant well.

"Ralph, dinner's ready: clams steamed in beer," Sarah said.

He lifted the lid from the pan and inhaled the aroma. "Wow, my favorite dish! And what's more, with our local Samuel Adams beer, I see."

They eagerly tucked into the food, and Ralph said, "You're such a wiz in the kitchen."

When they were finished eating, they worked together to clear the empty plates.

"Sarah, honey, we can start on dessert," he told her.

<hr>

After the meal and the dishes were finished, Ralph gave her a kiss. "You smell great," he whispered in her ear. He started smelling her neck and shoulders. Her scent was both fresh and sensual, with hints of pineapple, rose, and nutmeg. He then moved his hand along the back of her neck up to her hair and tugged it gently.

Sarah sensed his yearning for her. He breathed into her ear and murmured, "Sarah, honey, you're so damn beautiful." He kissed her neck, and the tension in her body rose. He began to stroke her and caressed her breasts. They felt soft and smooth. He took her in his arms and cuddled her.

She was now really turned on, reciprocating this embrace with a long kiss.

"Sarah, you've got such a sexy body." He started removing her clothes, and she took off his.

"Ralph, you know how much I want a baby with you …"

Four weeks later, Sarah met her friend Liliana in the cozy surroundings of Emmet's Irish Pub in Boston.

"You look really happy, Sarah," said Liliana.

"You bet," she replied. "And there's a reason why."

"Tell me! I wanna know everything!"

"Well, you can be the first to know: Ralph and I are trying for a baby."

"That's fantastic news!"

"We're both really looking forward to it. Now that we're both in our midthirties, we think the time has come."

"I'm super happy for you!"

Sarah sipped her drink and asked, "How are things with your son?"

"He's now two months old, and he's just the most wonderful thing that's ever happened to me. You'll be feeling the same thing soon. I just know you will."

Ten months and countless sex sessions later, Sarah was over at Liliana's place. Liliana was gushing about the joys of dirty diapers and sleepless nights, about the *dada laugh* then *poopoop my little guyguyguy just look how sweet he poops everything out again* …

"Hey, Sarah, why are you leaving?"

"Oh, nothing. I, erm, see you next week."

Sarah made her way home and prepared dinner routinely.

"That meal was delicious, Sarah. Should we have dessert?" asked Ralph.

"No, I don't feel like it."

That gave Ralph a start. "Is something wrong?"

"I'm already outside my fertile window," she said irritably.

"Oh, okay." Ralph was disillusioned and looked taken aback. That didn't escape Sarah.

"Sorry to react like that, I'm just frustrated we've not had any luck."

He then clasped her hand tightly. "I understand. I'm not happy about it either."

"Maybe there's something wrong?" she asked.

Ralph thought about it and then suggested, "The uncertainty's getting the better of us. Let's go have a fertility checkup."

"That's a great idea," said Sarah, somewhat relieved.

"Massachusetts General Hospital has a fertility center. We can get tested there. Then we'll be sure."

Following the tests, Sarah and Ralph had an appointment with the center's fertility specialist. The doctor warmly invited them into his office. "Sarah, Ralph, please take a seat."

They sat down with trepidation as the doctor began. "Let's get to the point," he told them. "I have the test results here. There's nothing indicating infertility, neither in Sarah, nor in you Ralph. What we suspect is that Sarah's ovulation is occurring intermittently, given the irregular periods. To remedy this, I recommend a course of hormone therapy. That will see to regulate ovulation stimulation and increase the chances of pregnancy."

"Thank you, Doctor. That's a weight off our shoulders," answered Sarah. "We both really want a baby. What's the likelihood the treatment will succeed?"

"That's down to individual circumstances. Eighty percent of

women with irregular or absent menstruation ovulate following the treatment. After a three-month course, fifty percent become pregnant."

"What does the course involve?" asked Sarah.

"With this, you take the medicine called clomiphene citrate. This tablet-form medication stimulates the production of various hormones responsible for ovulation. During the treatment, it's regularly checked in hospital that your ovaries aren't producing too many egg cells. You can't take the medicine for longer than three months since long-term risks are associated. I can prescribe it for six months, but after the first three months, you'll have to stop for one month in between treatments."

"Okay. I'm ready," said Sarah, full of hope.

———

One month later, Sarah's father, Gary Olson, came to visit her and Ralph. Sarah started talking effusively about Ralph and her work at the physio practice.

"You're very emotional, Sarah. I'm not used to this from you."

"It's because of the hormones, Dad. I'm taking medicine to get pregnant. We really want a baby, but it's not happening on its own."

Gary shook his head. "Sarah, what on earth are you doing?"

"What do you mean, Dad?"

"Well, you know how much I love nature. If it were possible, I'd give nature back to nature. Humans are behind everything that's going wrong with the world: overpopulation, terrorism, hate and envy, resource depletion, pollution, woodlands and rain forests disappearing, animal and plant species going extinct, monocultures, global warming, waste, mountains of garbage … People have become a disease. It's the plant and animal kingdom versus humanity. It would be better for humans to disappear rather than to procreate."

"And that means you're against us wanting a baby? Dad, I don't agree with your ideas one bit. They horrify me. Has it even occurred to you that only a part of humanity is responsible for what's wrong with the world? Most people want the best for the planet. Does that mean we have to be punished?"

Sarah burst into tears. Ralph comforted her and said forcefully, "Gary, don't you think your ideas are the height of hypocrisy for someone who's had a child himself? Why not allow your own daughter this happiness now?"

Gary said nothing and left.

⚬⚬⚬

Two months later, Sarah realized that her periods had stopped. That might mean a possible pregnancy! To make sure, she bought a pregnancy test from the pharmacy.

At home, she hurriedly peed into a jar and put the dipstick into the urine sample. She waited for the result impatiently as the seconds dragged on.

After one minute, the stick displayed two lines. She was pregnant! A sense of euphoria overwhelmed her. She grabbed her cell phone and called Ralph straightaway.

"Ralph, I'm pregnant!"

"Wow! Sarah, that's fantastic news! Are you sure?"

"Yeah, honey, the result of the pregnancy test is crystal clear! Finally, after trying for all those months. I'm over the moon."

"I'm really happy too, Sarah! We're having our first baby! You'll be a mommy and I'll be a daddy. Are you going to make an appointment with the doctor?"

"Of course. I'm going to call right now!"

⚬⚬⚬

The next day, Sarah and Ralph went to the doctor.

"I'll take a blood sample from you for good measure, Sarah. It's just a little pin prick. The blood test results will confirm you're pregnant. In the meantime, here's some great advice for during pregnancy. Eat healthy food. Read more about that in this brochure. Are you taking folic acid yet? Get some from the drugstore or pharmacy and start on that today. You don't need a prescription. By taking folic acid, also known as vitamin B11, the baby has less chance of nervous-system disorders. See the litter box as a potential hazard from now on, and don't start gardening like crazy without gloves or making mud pies in the sandbox, because of the risk for toxoplasmosis infection. This goes without saying, but no cigarettes, and, of course, steer clear from alcohol from now on. Not even a half glass to celebrate. And stay out of smoke-filled spaces."

Sarah called the doctor the following day. He had good news. "I have the result of the blood test here. You're well and truly pregnant, Sarah. Congratulations!"

"Thank you, Doctor! I'm overjoyed. I'm now taking the folic acid just like you recommended."

"Excellent! So, I suggest we see each other every four weeks for a checkup. I'll put the next appointment in my calendar."

The ecstatic couple already started making plans for the future baby. "We can empty out the junk room and turn it into a kid's room," said Ralph.

"That's a great idea! I'd like to pick out new wallpaper for there this weekend. Something colorful. You wanna come with me?"

"You bet! Wallpaper City in Roslindale has plenty to choose from. That's just over three miles from here."

That Saturday, Ralph and Sarah visited the store.

"Hello there, and how can I be of service today?" asked the store assistant.

"We're looking for cute wallpaper for a kid's room."

"Then you've come to the right place! Here we have our range of colorful and cheery children's wallpaper. We've got ones inspired by Charlie Brown and Snoopy, the Smurfs, lemurs in the jungle or fun dinosaurs."

"Oh, this one with Manny, Sid, Diego, and Scrat from *Ice Age*!" said Sarah.

"Definitely, we love those films," said Ralph. "Let's take that one."

"An excellent choice!" the store assistant agreed.

With her head in the clouds, Sarah hugged Ralph and gave him a big kiss.

Sarah started bleeding twelve days later. She started having back pain and stomach cramps at the same time. Intensely startled and unnerved, Ralph and Sarah decided to drive to the hospital's ER. An ultrasound performed there revealed that Sarah had had a miscarriage. The emergency doctor attempted to reassure the couple, "A miscarriage is usually down to a natural and spontaneous termination of a pregnancy presenting chromosomal abnormality. It's rarely caused by a uterus abnormality or an infectious disease. Any woman can have a miscarriage, even if they don't have any fertility problems. Women under twenty have a twelve percent chance of a miscarriage, and with women over forty, that's twenty-six percent."

"I just feel so sad," said Sarah. "What should I do now?"

"In general, no treatment is required for a miscarriage. The fetus and the remaining tissue were ejected from you naturally. However, many women do in fact suffer psychological effects, which can often be quite intense. If you'd like, I can prescribe you a few sessions with a therapist."

"I just want a baby so much. Is that still possible?"

"It's very likely. I see you were taking a round of hormones to get pregnant. The best thing now is to wait a month and then start taking them again for three months, under the fertility specialist's supervision."

Dejected, the couple drove home. Sarah didn't say a word the entire journey. She was fighting off the pain she still felt in her back and stomach. Once home, she passed by the emptied junk room. Her eyes welled up with tears. She went to the bedroom and collapsed onto the bed. She sobbed.

"Oh, Ralph, I'm so depressed. I was so looking forward to our baby. It wasn't meant to be. What did I do wrong?"

Ralph sat down beside her and placed his hand on her shoulder. "Sweetheart, you aren't to blame. It's a cruel trick of nature. The fetus wasn't viable."

"I know, but this loss is so hard to accept. Please hold me."

Ralph took her into his arms tightly. "The most important thing is you still have a chance to get pregnant. That doctor said you can resume the hormone treatment in a month."

Over the next few days, Sarah dragged herself along through her household chores, more robotically than human. Even when the pain disappeared and after two days she could go back to work, she still felt despondent and broken. She took comfort in her loving husband and in the thought of becoming pregnant once again. She started the hormones treatment again after a month, hopeful that things would go right this time. Ralph was behind her all the way, and they shared many moments of passion. Two months later, Sarah and Ralph were back at the fertility specialist.

"I can confirm that pregnancy has not yet occurred, despite the hormone treatment," the doctor said.

"Hearing that isn't easy, Doctor. I'm feeling desperate," said Sarah. "Sometimes I wonder if I'm brave enough to keep going because of the side effects. They've got me on an emotional roller coaster. One minute I'm jumping into the air; the next I'm down in the dumps."

"I suggest we repeat a few tests to be sure. This means I'll need to take some blood from you again. We'll know the results in three days."

One week later, Ralph was at the bar of the Bukowski Tavern in Boston, his usual place.

"So? Been to the doctor again?" asked his friend Brian, the bar owner.

"Ugh."

"So, yeah. What did he say?"

"That Sarah's become infertile. Something with the thyroid gland."

"Oh."

"Yeah, oh."

"And so you're giving up? Isn't there something you can do, hormones or something? A different doctor?"

Ralph didn't reply but stared into his glass.

"Here, have another one. How's Sarah coping?"

"Well, you know Sarah. Crying and stuff. It'll all blow over. It just has to."

Fifteen minutes later, Ralph left for home. Once there, he found Sarah asleep in bed, despite it being only six in the evening. That wasn't like her at all. Alarmed, he bent down to her.

"Hey, Sarah … Sarah?" There was no response. "Sarah, honey, please wake up!" Still no movement.

He carefully held her shoulder and shook it gently, but she wouldn't wake up. The bedside table then caught his eye. On it was a box of half-empty sleeping pills. Ralph's heart sank. Signs all pointed to an attempted suicide by overdose! Ralph swore, scrambled for his cell phone, and called an ambulance right away.

"Hello, how can we help you today?" said a female voice at the other end of the line.

"I can't wake up my wife. She's taken a heap of sleeping pills!"

"I'll send an ambulance immediately, sir. What's the address?"

"Six Adelaide Street, Jamaica Plain, Boston."

The minutes seemed like hours. Then, finally, the ambulance arrived. It took Sarah to the hospital, where the doctors were able to pump her stomach—just in the nick of time. Ralph was with her when she finally woke.

"Mmm, where am I?" she asked.

"Sarah, sweetheart, you're at the hospital."

"I remember … infertile. Sleeping … forever."

"You really scared me there, Sarah. Why?"

"Oh, Ralph, I felt so bad that I didn't want to carry on living."

"We'll get through this together, honey. How do you feel now?"

"Still groggy from the pills."

At that same moment, another shaken couple left the fertility center. The doctor mumbled, "Damn. That's now the sixth young woman from Boston who turns out to be infertile in the same way in two weeks. Could this just be a coincidence, or is it something more?"

CHAPTER 2

"**M**r. President, if we don't do something, in a hundred years, there'll be no people left!" came the alarming words of Ian Griffith, Secretary of Health and Human Services.

President Ron J. Adams looked up with astonishment from behind his oak desk in the Oval Office. There stood Ian, who was usually calm and collected, but now seemed to be a nervous wreck.

"That's a grave statement, Ian," the president said. "What exactly do you mean?"

"Infertile. They're becoming infertile. Women, I mean. All of them!"

"*Infertile?* Ian, sit down," he said before pressing a button on the intercom. "Erm, Maureen, please cancel all my calls—even the red one—and have Ambassador Sergejev wait. I mustn't be disturbed right now." He turned his attention back to Ian. "What the hell do you mean?"

"Here's a report by epidemiologist Shira Fox from our Centers for Disease Control and Prevention (CDC). She doesn't pull any punches. There's an epidemic spreading. Women are becoming infertile in both America and Europe. The number of women requesting fertility tests is rising, and the results are the same: infertile. The number of births in cities are also declining. If it carries on this way, we have to fear the worst for the human race's survival."

The president looked at Ian anxiously. "That really does

sound serious. Any clue how this could happen? I mean, these things don't crop up by themselves, do they?"

"No, Mr. President. Our scientists suspect an infectious disease. But right now, we're completely in the dark."

"Damn it, just when the North Koreans are at it again. Like I didn't already have enough on my plate. Have other scientists already confirmed this?"

"Yes, our statistical services were also behind the report. It's group work with Shira Fox having supervised our very best bioscientists."

The president picked up the unsettling report and skimmed over the summary: Falling birth rates. Recommendations. Utmost priority. Global health alert. Code orange. Finally, he said firmly, "Ian, set up an urgent meeting with Shira Fox so we can discuss this with her and put appropriate measures in place."

"Yes, sir, Mr. President!"

―――∞∞∞―――

Shira Fox strolled wearily out of Atlanta university's sleek auditorium. Three hours of listening to a symposium on epidemics throughout the ages was exhausting, and the fact she'd needed the restroom for quite some time didn't improve matters. While hurrying to the ladies' room, she passed by the reception room and noticed Alexander Bullock, one of the speakers, savoring a glass of single-malt whiskey. She chuckled to herself, thinking about how he looked just like some clichéd university professor— balding head, glasses, and a gray beard.

She washed her hands, checked in the mirror that she looked presentable enough, winked her approval, and strode to the reception room.

I must admit, she thought, remembering the professors who taught her as a young student, *the old guy commands respect. Charisma is something you either have, or you don't. He's got it, and he certainly knows how to use it.* Despite having graduated five years earlier, she still felt wet behind the ears when comparing herself to

Bullock. He wasn't just a professor of classical languages but also an authority on the world's oldest written texts.

To mask her unease, she decided to take a glass of champagne and make her way unobtrusively to where Bullock was standing, deep in conversation with a pair of students who were hanging on his every word as if he were the latest guru.

The wide-eyed students made Shira laugh to herself, which certainly helped, since it somewhat diluted her nervousness in talking with this man, who was so revered in academic circles.

What she wanted to ask him and how she'd do so flashed through her mind. He had something of an epicurean and a fatherly figure about him; he looked pleasant and was most likely a nice person. Mustering all her courage, she resolved to take the plunge.

"Erm, Professor Bullock?"

The old man turned around, seeking out the person addressing him. To his surprise, he saw a beautiful young woman standing there. She had long brown hair, dimples in her cheeks, and wore a smart suit.

"Young lady? Are we already acquainted?" asked Bullock, charmed by the female company.

"Professor, my name is Shira Fox, and I'd really appreciate it if you'd grant me a couple of minutes of your time."

A broad grin spread over Bullock's face. "What did you think of my lecture?" he asked.

"It was fascinating. It struck me that the impact of the plague of Justinian on Byzantine society displays so much similarity with the impact of contemporary epidemics. You also very briefly mentioned the infertility epidemic during the Sumerian civilization. Could you tell me a bit more about that?"

Bullock seemed taken aback by her question. "That epidemic is a myth. Little is known about it. Wouldn't you rather hear about the ten plagues of Egypt? I can tell you everything about those." He knew how to make an impression on his audience with the often-astonishing explanation of those ten plagues.

Shira looked at him doubtfully. *Here we go*, she thought.

Typical male! Evasive answers. Does he think I'm just some dumb chick? I'm not falling for it. "No, I already know the ten plagues rather well due to my profession," she responded firmly. "But thanks anyway." She finished off her champagne, turned around, and made a move to leave.

It was now she who fascinated him instead of vice versa. "Hey, Shira, did I say something wrong?"

"I'm going for another drink, Professor."

"Allow me. What would you like?"

"A fruit juice is fine."

He fetched the desired drink and swiftly returned to Shira. "You just mentioned your profession. What is it?"

"I'm an epidemiologist at the CDC."

"I see. Now I understand why you're already so familiar with the ten plagues of Egypt."

"However, the infertility epidemic is still a mystery to me. There's been no other such epidemic since the Sumerian case. Could you tell me about it, please?"

Because the female attention he was receiving stroked his vanity, Bullock complied with her request. "As you wish."

He put down his glass and took hold of the reception table as if it were an auditorium podium.

"That epidemic is embedded in a mythological narrative from the Sumerian culture. Sumerian culture is one of the most ancient civilizations we know of. It dated from 3800 to 2000 before Christ and was located in Mesopotamia, the land between the Tigris and the Euphrates."

"The land between two rivers," Shira interrupted. "Present-day Iraq, isn't it?" She beamed as she spoke.

"Correct! I see you know your history!" Bullock was now visibly over the moon with Shira's ready knowledge and eagerly resumed his academic discourse. "The Sumerians formed a cradle of civilization. They invented writing, the wheel, the plow, irrigation, the twenty-four-hour day, and the first city states. In 1900, archaeological excavations took place in Nippur, Iraq. The excavations were led by a compatriot, the American John

Henry Haynes of the University of Pennsylvania. Unearthed in the temple's library were thousands of clay tablets, inscribed with Sumerian cuneiform writing. Much of what we know about Sumerian literature today comes from that discovery."

"Quite a job for translators!"

"Indeed. All the more because Sumerian cuneiform could not be read at the outset. This required a lengthy process of searching, comparing with other ancient languages, and attempts at translation. Scholars from several countries collaborated on this.

"The French scholar François Thureau-Dangin, for instance, played a pivotal role in translating Sumerian cuneiform," the professor digressed. He quickly sipped from his glass, as if about to embark on a long, didactic lecture. "The whiskey they have here's splendid …"

Shira sighed. "Great, but what about the epidemic?"

Her gaze let slip a hint of impatience that didn't escape Alexander. He abandoned his hobbyhorse and got to the nub. "Ah, well, some of the clay tablets from Nippur contain the story of the goddess Inanna's descent to the underworld. That's the story featuring the infertility epidemic."

"I'm all ears," said Shira intently.

All of a sudden, Shira was approached by a man in a dark suit, who had just arrived. "Ms. Shira Fox? My name is Alan. I'm a security officer for the president of the United States. I've been instructed to take you to the president as quickly as possible for an emergency meeting, relating to your report. Would you follow me, please?"

"Erm, of course. Let me just say goodbye to the professor." She turned to Alexander. "Professor, I can't stay any longer, but I'll get in touch with you for the rest of the story. Bye for now!"

Before the professor could even say anything, she had vanished.

The flight from Atlanta to Washington went smoothly. Shira was on time for her meeting with the president and Ian Griffith. Her alarming report had seemingly hit the mark.

While at first she was anxious about what the consequences of her report might be, during the flight she was able to prepare herself for the impending meeting, and her nerves were already much calmer. It was either sink or swim now, she thought. She confidently entered the large meeting room in the White House where Ian Griffith was waiting and greeted her.

"Hello, Shira, how was your journey?"

"All good, Mr. Griffith. You planned it all out: taxis, air tickets, hotel, even a personal escort from a security officer. I feel just like a VIP."

"It was also necessary in this case. As you'll understand."

"Yes, my report—" she started, but Ian cut her off.

"It shocked us immensely. But please, have something to drink while we wait for the president. He's always promptly on time."

"I see there's a projector here, but I don't have a presentation with me."

"Please don't worry. I've already had a presentation made up of your report's most important parts. We'll be able to project that presentation."

The president made his entrance at the time scheduled. Shira knew him only from television and online, and he'd made a good impression on her. He took his presidency seriously. The fact that he had illustrious ancestors, including two ex-presidents, made her trust him all the more. Now, seeing him in the flesh, that impression was confirmed. He had a stately bearing, a presidential allure, and immediately put her at ease.

"Ms. Shira Fox," the president said. "I'm glad you could come at such short notice to explain your explosive report. It seems we have no time to lose."

"That's right, Mr. President!" Shira answered.

"Well, Ian, start the presentation," the president said. "Shira, go ahead."

And she did. "The statistics services track birth rates meticulously; this is the number of births per annum, per thousand residents. This figure is calculated per city, per state, and per country. Normally, the birth rate is at around 13.42 percent for the United States. However, in recent months this has been falling everywhere, and more markedly so in major cities. For Washington, DC, the birth rate is currently only 12.78 percent

"A fluctuation in the birth rate. Doesn't that often occur?" asked the president.

"That's true, but a drop across the board in the United States and Europe is unprecedented. That can no longer be a coincidence. Something abnormal is happening here."

"And there's no chance of an error in the statistics?" he asked.

"An error might occur for one single location, but not for dozens of locations in the United States and in Europe simultaneously," Shira responded. "On top of that, the number of women trying for babies who turn out to be infertile is on the rise everywhere, particularly in major cities. In Washington, DC, there's an increase of no less than sixteen percent.

"These graphs reveal that an infertility epidemic commenced about two years ago. The phenomenon started out in big cities such as New York, Boston, Philadelphia, Washington, DC, Chicago, New Orleans, Atlanta, San Francisco, Los Angeles, London, Paris, Brussels, and so on. Although the onset wasn't so pronounced, we can now make out a trend. The symptoms have spread all over the United States and Europe. We estimate that around three percent of women in the United States and Europe are affected by this. In major cities, this can go as high as thirty percent."

"This is extremely serious, Shira," said the president. "Do we know the cause?"

"Unfortunately not, Mr. President. We have, however, established that the women becoming infertile are suffering from an immunological problem—thyroid antibodies in the blood, to be specific. This means the fetus is rejected following conception.

From the way the epidemic is spreading, we can calculate that this most likely involves an infectious disease."

"What about other possible causes? I'm thinking climate change, pollution, a biochemical attack," the president suggested.

"We still can't rule anything out right now. Further research will be required."

"This is highly distrusting. What are the epidemic's long-term consequences?" the president asked.

"I have a simulation of the disorder's progression here," she said. "According to the trend, for every infected person we see now, there will be ten more infected people in four months' time. That means, after a year, we have a factor of one thousand. If we don't act, the birth rate in the United States will drop to zero within one year and three months. In major cities, this will already have happened within nine months. In Europe, this will have occurred within only a year and a half, since the population there is greater."

"I'm horrified," said the president. "An appalling prospect. An unprecedented disaster for the people, our economy, and our way of life. This would mean humanity's extinction. Is this disease irreversible, or is the infertility permanent?"

"As it stands, we've established that the reproductive organs of the women becoming infertile have remained intact. That indicates the disease might be reversible with the right medication."

"However, that medication hasn't been found yet?" he asked.

"No. And it might take a long time before one is found. Just look at AIDS. There still isn't a cure after all these years. Researching and developing new medicines is slow, uncertain, and extremely expensive."

"Shira, what's your advice? Is there a disaster plan available?"

"Yes, Mr. President. Our CDC has devised a disaster plan for tackling large-scale epidemics called Alarm Code Orange. I propose activating this plan."

"What does it entail?"

"There are various aspects. First of all, we must ascertain

the cause of the epidemic and find a remedy, whatever the cost. The plan also requires all government medical laboratories to give this top priority. They will also have to provide maximum cooperation by publishing information and results immediately."

"How do we deal with private laboratories?"

"Different rules apply to private labs. The companies' intellectual properties must be protected to encourage investments in innovation. Competition should be allowed between the pharmaceutical industries to find an effective medicine first. The Food and Drug Administration will then compare the proposed medicines in terms of performance and safety. The current approval procedure for medicines is way too laborious. An accelerated approval procedure will be followed, so that the medicines can be released much more quickly."

"What are the other implications of the plan?"

"All human travel and face-to-face interactions must be limited to those strictly necessary, to counteract further infection," she explained.

"Please define *strictly necessary*."

"In this case, we mean travel and interaction required to keep our economy, education, and the emergency services going. For meetings, modern tools such as telephones, videoconferencing, and chat should be used as much as possible. Where feasible, working from home or remote working is recommended. To favor these telecommunications above other online traffic, internet providers will suppress all nonessential traffic on the web."

"How can that happen in practice, Shira?"

"A list of websites and data traffic to be blocked has already been drawn up. This list is comparable to what major companies already block with their firewalls."

"What do we do about social media?"

"Social media and email are not blocked, to allow people to continue communicating. Applications eating up too much network capacity, such as online video games, YouTube, and similar online video services will nevertheless be blocked to free up space for the increased telecommunication demands."

"Drastic measures, Shira! A lot of people aren't going to like it. But I'm afraid we have no other option."

"That's right, Mr. President. Given the special circumstances we're in, there is no alternative. However, the plan will be assessed every month and adjusted where necessary to take the epidemic's development and people's needs into account."

The president turned to Ian. "Ian, we have to consult with the most important stakeholders. Convene a meeting as soon as possible with myself, Shira, yourself, the vice president, the secretary of state, the secretary of homeland security, the secretary of commerce, the secretary of the interior, the secretary of education, and the national security advisor, so we can ask for their advice and support. This has the highest priority!"

This meeting took place the next day. Shira shared her report once again. The plan and its implications were deliberated. Shira also argued for schools, hospitality establishments, and museums to close, and for mass events and travel to be prohibited. Even so, the other attendees balked at such extreme measures because the epidemic's cause was still unknown. They also argued about the huge impact on the economic and cultural sectors. The restrictions on the internet were, however, accepted; as well as a ban on gatherings of over a thousand people.

Ian made an interesting suggestion. "I'd like to propose involving the World Health Organization. The WHO operates globally, has funds for emergency situations, and can oversee the collaboration with our European allies."

"An excellent suggestion," said the president. "I'm counting on you to get the ball rolling! In the public's best interest, I will activate the Alarm Code Orange disaster plan, according to the assessments made today. Instruct our CDC to distribute all available information to our laboratories and to coordinate all efforts within the United States. Ms. Fox should assume a key role in this."

The secretary of state, in charge of foreign policy, added, "We shouldn't rule out this involving a biological attack from an enemy power. I will therefore call on our intelligence services to step up their activities."

Ian asked, "What about the public and the press? Are we notifying them? Newspaper articles have recently been appearing, discussing the rising number of infertility examinations. There is nothing alarming being reported yet, but I can see that changing in the near future."

"We can't keep this a secret," answered the president. "There'll be too many people involved in our activities."

"That's true, and the press will be getting wind of it in no time," Ian noticed.

"At the same time, we mustn't sow panic. I'm therefore asking Josh Gordon, our press secretary, to hold a press conference in order to inform the press and public."

"I'll give him Shira's report now," Ian said, "so we can prepare together."

"Have the press conference broadcast through live streaming online so we're setting a good example from word go," said the president. "I'll also use the Situation Room for a video conference with the world's friendly heads of state and governments, to notify them and explain the imminent collaboration."

A week later, the press conference commenced, entitled "Press Briefing by Secretary of Health and Human Services Ian Griffith," streamed live from the White House. Ian presented the participants an array of colorful graphs. He concluded, "The graphs reveal that around two years ago, an infertility epidemic commenced. Although the onset wasn't so pronounced, we can now see a trend. The disease spread all over the United States and Europe. We estimate that around three percent of women in the United States and Europe are infected by the illness. The president believes this poses a potential threat to the population. For this reason, he has activated the Alarm Code Orange disaster plan. This plan instructs the CDC to coordinate medical laboratories in the United States in seeking out the cause and finding a solution. We are also concurrently collaborating with the WHO to guide a worldwide search. You may now ask questions using the chat functionality."

"Can this be boiled down to a terrorist attack with radioactive radiation, for instance?" asked a journalist.

"There's nothing indicating this. No increase in radioactivity has been measured anywhere," answered Ian.

"Could nuclear tests be the cause of the rising infertility?" asked another journalist.

"Same answer."

"Could this be an act of biological warfare by the Russians, the Chinese, or the North Koreans?"

"There's nothing pointing to this, no event from our intelligence services," Ian answered. "We even suspect that this epidemic is affecting people in Russia and China."

"How can we make sure we don't catch the disease?"

"We still don't know how the disease is spread. We therefore don't know the preventative measures. The Alarm Code Orange disaster plan involves restricting all human travel and face-to-face interactions, to counteract further infection. Schools, bars and restaurants, and museums are remaining open, and mass events and travel can continue while the cause of the disease is unknown. Gatherings of over one thousand people are prohibited. Meetings must take place by telephone, video conference, or chat. Working from home and remote working are recommended. To be able to meet the increased telecommunication needs, all nonessential web traffic will be blocked."

"Can infected people be put into quarantine?"

"That just isn't feasible. This concerns huge numbers, and we know neither exactly who has the disease nor who hasn't."

"Are birth rates from outside the United States and Europe known?"

"No, not yet, although we're hoping to get those soon through the WHO."

"How will this affect our economy?"

ERESHKIGAL'S VENGEANCE

"Well, if this persists, local economies and the global economy will have to make do with fewer people, both employees and consumers. But let's avoid doom-mongering. We're confident that our joint medical laboratories will find a cure for this epidemic."

"Could the disease be a solution for overpopulation?" quipped a journalist.

"No, planned birth control is a solution for overpopulation, not an epidemic," Ian answered curtly.

"Precisely what web traffic is going to be blocked?"

"The traffic to be blocked is nonessential traffic that takes up lots of bandwidth, such as torrent downloads, visits to pornographic sites, online video games, YouTube, and similar online video services. A complete list is being published soon on the White House website. This will be a live list, regularly adjusted according to the requirements. Social media and email are being kept in place, so that people can continue communicating online."

"How will that web traffic be blocked?"

"That will happen by blocking certain URLs and certain types of data traffic in the internet providers' firewalls."

"What if internet providers refuse to cooperate?"

"They'll be obligated to cooperate. A bill is currently being drawn up."

"That's highly drastic! Who's going to manage the list of websites and data traffic to be blocked?"

"A number of companies specialized in blocking websites and data traffic will see to managing this, based on government policy and guidelines. This is nothing new. Blocking already occurs in the firewalls of major companies and organizations, preventing employees from visiting certain websites."

"What about citizens' rights to visit whatever websites they want? There'll be heavy protests against these measures."

"I understand that. Nevertheless, public-health interests supersede individual's freedoms in this instance."

Mere moments after the press conference, the media was already brimming with information available on the epidemic, and the government's measures. The titles read: "Global Pandemic Underway, Cause of Infertility Unknown," "WHO and CDC Tackle Infertility Disease," and "Unprecedented Restrictions on Internet." There were howling protests on social media against the far-reaching internet restrictions. The government was accused of exploiting the epidemic to push these limitations through. Some people even went as far as to claim the government had invented the epidemic, so as to curb the World Wide Web. Archconservatives in turn welcomed the measures with open arms: away with illegal downloads, porn, and online gaming.

Shira read the reports in the media and felt tremendous responsibility for what was happening. Not only would she have to coordinate all the efforts against the epidemic from now on, but she was also behind the Alarm Code Orange disaster plan and its measures that were now being so fiercely debated. At the same time, she also felt pride that she could make a useful contribution to public health both in the United States and worldwide. She thought about her father and how proud he would have been of her, had he still been alive.

Her parents had been socially engaged people. They had provided a village in Nicaragua with water and soap, as part of the WaterAid hygiene program. They hadn't been afraid to roll up their sleeves, build water pumps and toilets, and to live a life of adventure in Central America. This meant that, as a child, Shira had learned to help others, which later influenced her when deciding what to study.

Shira's father had died in a car accident when she was six. That event affected her deeply because she loved her father dearly. Her mother did not have a good relationship with her father at the time of the accident and forbade her from crying for him. Shira had bottled up the pain of the loss instead of being able to mourn.

The lack of a father figure meant she had been self-reliant since a young age. She was also the eldest child and always had to look after her younger brother while her mother went to work. She had therefore grown up and become independent early on, and was a touch fanatical about organizing and caring for others.

When she was older, Shira had been awarded a scholarship to pursue her studies. She had made a point of studying fastidiously, gaining good grades, and not having to repeat a single year in school. After studying medicine, she specialized in epidemiology. Because she had achieved such outstanding results, she was able to start out as a researcher at the CDC. Her strong character and dedication meant that, within a few years, she had worked up to becoming a planner and the head epidemiologist. A downside of all this was that there wasn't yet any man in her life. This was because most were put off by enterprising and independent women. However, she still held out hope for a proper relationship. It was simply a question of finding the right man, she thought.

CHAPTER 3

Shira recalled Professor Alexander Bullock and his Sumerian story. She found his contact details in the brochure from the symposium. He worked in the Babylonia section of the Museum for Anthropology and Archeology at the University of Pennsylvania. She decided to call him.

"Hello, Professor," she said when he answered the phone, "this is Shira Fox, epidemiologist with the CDC."

"Hello. How might I be of assistance?"

"Do you remember the recent symposium, Epidemics throughout the Ages?"

"Certainly. I was one of the speakers."

"Well, I was the woman you spoke to about a Sumerian myth but who suddenly had to leave. I'd really like to know the rest of the story."

"How could I ever forget? A man in black came out of the blue and whisked you away for an urgent meeting with the president! Such a nerve. I was left in the lurch. And there we were, having a pleasant chat about one of my favorite subjects. Thankfully, I was able to wash down that disappointment with a nice glass of whiskey."

"My apologies. The report I'd written caused a great deal of commotion up in the highest circles, and the president urgently wanted to hear my recommendations. I assume you'll have already heard about the current epidemic?"

"I'll say. The media's full of it—a global pandemic. Restrictions on the internet. My lectures on YouTube are blocked. What's to become of us all?"

"The situation is indeed serious. That's why we're doing our utmost to find the cause and any possible solutions. The Sumerian story might help."

"Aha! Now the cat's out of the bag. I'm glad you thought of me. The lessons from the past, isn't it? You see, an old fogy like me can still come in handy.

"Anyway, I shall send you all the details about the ancient infertility epidemic, given that there might be a connection with the current one. I contributed toward the most recent translation of this into English myself. While that was certainly no easy feat, the result is readable. What's your email address? I'll send you the document today with the translation."

Shira told him her address. *Alexander must surely know that I'm behind his YouTube videos being blocked. I'll just keep that information to myself,* she thought following the call.

Alexander sent her the following message:

Dear Shira,

I'm delighted to be able to help you. From the translation of the clay tablets with cuneiform text found in Iraq to date, the following narrative can be reconstructed:

In the very earliest of days, the god of wisdom, Enki, set out in his boat. He was heading for the underworld, there to impregnate the queen of the underworld, Ereshkigal. The fruit of this copulation between Enki and Ereshkigal was the huluppu tree that arose on the banks of the Euphrates. But then, suddenly, a storm broke out and the sapling huluppu was uprooted and swept away by the water. Fortunately, the young Inanna was close by. She rescued the tree and planted it in her sacred garden, dreaming of how this tree would later provide her a throne and a bed.

The tree grew and blossomed. However, many years later, a serpent nestled itself unseen into the tree's roots. And then the Anzu bird nested in the crown unnoticed. And to make matters worse, the dark Lilith, notorious devourer of men and babies, secretly built her house in the huluppu tree's trunk. Inanna was always bright and full of joy, but when she discovered this, she wailed. Inanna cried hot tears and broke into a loud lamentation.

The god An took possession of the heavens.

Enlil took possession of the earth.

My sister Ereshkigal took possession of the underworld.

Enki sailed to the underworld, after which I rescued the huluppu tree myself. There was no magnificent throne and no regal bed for me, only a tree where the serpent, the calamitous bird, and the dreaded Lilith have nestled.

How long before I can take my place on an exquisite throne? How long before I can lie down on an immaculate bed?

When the day broke and her brother, the sun god Utu, awoke, she told him, sobbing, about what had befallen her beautiful huluppu tree. But Utu did not listen.

She then complained to Gilgamesh, the great Sumerian hero. And Gilgamesh paid heed of Inanna's lamentation. He donned his weaponry: armor weighing more than fifty pounds. He took his ax and slew the serpent, who knew no affection. He next drove out the Anzu bird. And he even chased the fierce Lilith from the tree. He then carved for Inanna a royal throne and a royal bed from the trunk.

Once the youthful Inanna reached adulthood, her awakening feminine power bestowed greater self-confidence. She realized that she needed "divine gifts" to establish herself as queen and to lead her people.

As soon as Inanna heard that Enki had returned home, she wished to visit him, adorned in her regal attire. On his part, Enki commanded his servant to receive Inanna as an equal and to show her respect.

Enki, the god of wisdom, and Inanna, who coveted the queenship so, drank beer together. They drank beer together until Enki, clouded by the drink, began to make Inanna a whole series of solemn promises. Enki promised Inanna priesthood and queenship. And Enki, clouded by drink, promised even more. He promised Inanna both her descent to the underworld and her return from whence.

He promised the capability to love. The gift of decision-making. He bequeathed her, clouded by drink, the sacred Mes—or the laws of the upper world. The sacred Mes contained maxims that spread art, crafts, and civilization, but could equally lay waste to cities.

He bestowed on her an elevated priesthood and the crown of queenship. He gifted her a measuring rod and measuring line. He granted her the truth, which would bring about the descent and return from the underworld. He offered her a sword, bow, and arrow. He presented her with black and colored garments and the skill of the sacred whore. He gave her the gift of speaking and the talent of singing. The capacity to travel and craftsmanship skills were hers. As were the shrewdness of judgment and the art of solace.

Enki, god of wisdom, gave all this to Inanna, who so coveted power. But after sleeping off his intoxication, Enki realized what he had done. He sent his servant to Inanna's boat to retrieve all the Mes, but Inanna thought otherwise!

Enki became angry, and dispatched a pair of giants to retrieve the Mes. But Inanna was powerful and too cunning for the giants. This made Enki even angrier, and he sent gruesome monsters out after her without success. Enki attempted to reclaim the Mes a full seven times. And yet, aided by her handmaiden Ninshubur, Inanna managed to sail her boat safely home. And when she unloaded the treasures, she discovered certain additional ones: the art of allurement and other feminine wiles.

Inanna was now the goddess of love, fertility, and martial arts, and she ruled over heaven and earth, thanks to Enki's gifts. Soon after, Inanna's brother Utu started to weave a bridal drape for Inanna.

"But I don't have a husband yet," complained Inanna.

"Dumuzi, the herdsman, wishes to be your husband," said Utu.

"No, the man of my heart is a nobleman," Inanna grumbled.

But Utu insisted, "Marry Dumuzi."

"Anything a nobleman gives you, I will give it better," boasted Dumuzi.

And Inanna yielded to his words and to his gifts. She adorned herself and invited him to her royal palace. At first, she opposed him, but soon the discussion progressed into passionate lovemaking. They celebrated life to its fullest. He brought her milk and honey in abundance. She gave him all the fervor she had in her. She made him into the god of vegetation and the harvest, and they celebrated love. They celebrated their sovereignty over the heavens and the earth, until Dumuzi was finally sated and wished to bask in the afterglow.

Inanna decided to share everything she had received from Enki with her people and to act as the benefactress of humanity. With the Mes, Inanna sailed in the celestial boat over the fresh-water abyss and founded her sacred city on Earth, Uruk. There, she civilized the people and heralded an age of peace and abundance.

The wise Enki resigned himself to this, blessing Inanna and declaring, "In the name of my power! In the name of my sacred temple! Let the Mes that you took remain in the city's sacred temple. Let the high priests pass their days at the sacred temple in song. Let the dwellers of your city know prosperity. Let the children of Uruk be joyous. Let the city of Uruk assume its prominent position."

Some years later, Ereshkigal, the goddess of the underworld, was enraged that the people made fewer offerings to her than to her younger sister, Inanna. Ereshkigal was not loved among the people, who were averse to the underworld, the realm of the dead. Ereshkigal felt rejected and abandoned. She therefore harbored a terrible grudge against Inanna and the people. To avenge herself on the people who had neglected her, Ereshkigal spread a plague of barrenness among them.

Inanna wished to reconcile with her sister and rival, Ereshkigal, and put an end to this plague. With these aims in mind, she wished to visit Ereshkigal in the underworld. Inanna donned her royal skirt, breastplate, and jewels that served as protection. She was ready to descend to the land of no return, the world of the dead and of darkness, presided over by her sister, the goddess Ereshkigal.

Through fear that her sister would kill her, Inanna gave instructions to her loyal handmaiden Ninshubur. "If I have not returned after three days and nights, you must lodge a protest for my return in the great hall of the gods."

Inanna descended. She approached the temple made of lapis lazuli. At the gateway, she encountered Neti, the guardian of the underworld. He asked her who she was and why she had come.

"I am Inanna, queen of the heavens, the place where the sun rises."

"If you are the queen of the heavens," Neti suggested, "the place where the sun rises, why then have you come to the land of no return?"

"I have come to reconcile with my sister, Ereshkigal, and to put an end to the plague of barrenness among my earthly subjects."

"Please wait while I report this to Ereshkigal," said Neti.

Neti was instructed to open the seven gates for the queen of the heavens, but to abide by the rules, and at each gate to remove an item of clothing from Inanna, a symbol of her power.

The first door opened, and Inanna's crown was taken from her.

"Why are you taking my crown?" she asked.

"Ask nothing. The laws of the underworld are perfect," said Neti.

The second gate opened, and the lapis lazuli beads were removed.

At the third gate, Neti removed the double string of beads from her breast.

At the fourth gate, the breast plate, and at the fifth the golden bracelet.

At the sixth gate, she had to abandon her measuring rod and measuring line, and at the seventh, finally, her royal garments. Each time, she asked, "Why?" and each time, Neti answered, "Because the laws of the underworld are perfect. Things are as they are."

After the seventh gate, Inanna stood naked and bowed before Ereshkigal's throne.

Ereshkigal was furious with her younger sister. She was furious and afraid because she feared that Inanna would also demand the throne of the underworld. She therefore brought Inanna before the Annunaki, the seven judges of the underworld.

The Annunaki surrounded Inanna and condemned her. Ereshkigal stared at Inanna with the eye of death, uttered words of ire against her, and let out an accusatory cry. Ereshkigal struck and impaled Inanna on a hook so that she died.

When, After three days and three nights, when Ninshubur had still not heard from her mistress, she sought help from the god Enlil, but to no avail. She then sought help from the god Nanna, who also refused.

"Were heaven and Earth not good enough? She also wanted the underworld!" responded first Enlil and then Nanna.

But Enki, the god of wisdom, took heed. It was ultimately he who, in a drunken spirit, had promised to Inanna both descent to the underworld and her return. He felt responsible. Sorrowful, he sought a solution to rescue Inanna and the people. From beneath his fingernail, Enki picked out some dirt and created from this two creatures: Kurgarra and Galatur. He handed to them the water of life and the food of life.

"Approach Ereshkigal as closely as you can," he commanded them. "And if Ereshkigal weeps, then weep with her. And if Ereshkigal wails, then wail with her. And if Ereshkigal sighs, then sigh with her."

Kurgarra and Galatur arrived in the underworld. As small as flies, they managed to creep through the cracks in the gates. They were unsure whether the *weeping and wailing from Ereshkigal was due to labor pangs or her death throes. They wept and wailed with her. For the first time in her life, Ereshkigal felt solidarity. This empathy made her relent. And seeing the sacrifice her sister had made also softened her heart. Ereshkigal stopped weeping and looked at them.*

"Who are you, and why do you moan, groan, and sigh with me?"

"We are Kurgarra and Galatur, created by the god Enki, to ease your suffering."

"I offer you my blessing. I also wish to give you a gift: the water, the river in its plenitude."

"This is most kind of you, goddess, but we do not desire the water."

"Let me then offer you the corn grains and the fields in harvest."

"Neither do we desire the corn grains, goddess."

"What do you want of me?"

"The rotting lump of meat on the hook in the wall, and a remedy for the plague of barrenness."

"While what you ask of me is not little, I consent on one condition: that someone comes to assume her place."

Kurgarra and Galatur lifted the putrid lump of meat and first poured over it the water of life and then the food of life.

Inanna then awoke from her suffering and slowly returned to life. At each of the gates they passed through, she was given back her items of clothing. On her return journey to the surface, she was accompanied by the Galla, minor demons from the underworld who sought someone to assume her place. The first to run to Inanna was Ninshubur.

"The handmaiden! Let us take the handmaiden," *screeched the Galla.*

ERESHKIGAL'S VENGEANCE

But Inanna did not wish that, since it was Ninshubur who had saved her. She had ensured Inanna could return to the surface.

All around, people cheered the return of the celestial queen. Inanna did not want the Galla to take anyone who had mourned her absence. They then encountered Shara, one of Inanna sons.

"No, not Shara," she cried. "Not Shara, my son."

"Lulal. Let us take Lulal to the underworld in her place," shrieked the Galla.

"Not Lulal, not my son," Inanna besought them.

Finally, they arrived at her palace. Her husband, Dumuzi, was lying on his couch, clad in fine clothing. Slave girls played flutes while he feasted and drank. Dumuzi had been making merry on his throne, while all that time she had been suffering in the underworld. She gave Dumuzi the eye of death. She declared to the Galla coolly, "You may take him."

But when the Galla went to seize him, he escaped. The powerful Dumuzi fled from the Galla, fearful as he was of the fate that awaited him. Dumuzi begged Utu, Inanna's brother, for help. "Transform my hands and feet into serpents so that I might evade the demons."

Dumuzi's hands transformed into serpents and his feet transformed into serpents.

Temporarily, Dumuzi's wish had been fulfilled. Nevertheless, the Galla pursued him and managed to take him prisoner. He was afraid and wept. He sought aid and solace from Geshtinanna, his sister.

Geshtinanna was prepared to share his fate. Calmly and with dignity, Inanna took Dumuzi by the hand and said, "Look, your sister, Geshtinanna, is prepared to share the stay in the underworld with *you. Half the year she will assume your place, while you can be here."*

This meant that Dumuzi, god of Vegetation, returned to his queen, Inanna, every year in spring. This six-monthly cycle ensured that the land retained its fertility and renewed annually.

Inanna shared the remedy for the barrenness epidemic with the high priests of her temple in Uruk. With this remedy, the priests cured the people and the animals.

In gratitude, the residents of Uruk erected a new stone temple in the city in joint honor of Inanna and Ereshkigal. They named this the House of Inanna and Ereshkigal, as well as the Temple of Heavens and the Underworld. Their sacrifices were now intended for both Inanna and for Ereshkigal so that both goddesses were satisfied.

Inanna's visit to Ereshkigal was viewed as the encounter between the creator and the destroyer, the shining and the darker side of the divine pair.

Kind regards,
Professor Alexander Bullock.

A fine tale, mumbled Shira, *but whether it's helped at all is highly questionable*. She called Alexander once again. "Hello, Professor, it's Shira Fox."

"Hello, Shira. Did you read the story?"

"I did indeed. It's a great story, but unfortunately, it's a tad vague on the remedy they applied. Is there any more known about the nature of the remedy or where we might be able to find it?"

"I'm afraid not. Certain clay tablets were damaged or incomplete, meaning parts of the story are missing."

"I understand. Should any more fragments be found, please be sure to let me know!"

"I most certainly will, Shira. You can count on it."

A few months later, the epidemic was raging with full intensity. The Earth has been hit by an unparalleled pandemic: the illness affected the fertility of all women infected. Given that the disease was highly contagious and caused no immediate damage, it spread among the population in no time, despite the disaster plan. This was because people were unable to remain at home all the time and occasionally had to travel to buy groceries or to transport goods. The infected women no longer gave birth to any babies. This led to a burgeoning sense of panic. The disaster started out in North America and Europe, made its way to South America and Asia, and extended throughout the entire world. The lack of new humans meant humanity's survival hung in the balance. The Middle East was, for a time, suffering less from the epidemic. According to Muslim extremists, this calamity was a punishment from Allah on nonbelievers. Obscure sects and fertility rituals ran rampant, enticing people in these times of heightened distress.

CHAPTER 4

Three years beforehand.

For a change, Gary Olson wasn't going to his usual workplace in Frederick County, Maryland. He was heading for Harvard University, near Boston. This was because he was enrolled on a five-day postgraduate course in the latest technologies for finding medicines against viruses.

It was the first day of the course. Gary made his way to the tall buildings and extensive grounds of Harvard Medical School. This school, founded back in 1782, was one of the oldest of its kind in the United States, and was renowned for its medical research.

Gary was unfamiliar with the place. Luckily, he'd thought to bring a map. The main building bordered a vast, tree-fringed square lawn. He climbed the steps to the building and cut across an imposing set of columns. A few corridors further was the auditorium. It reminded him of his bygone days as a student. He sought out a wastebasket to discard a leaflet about God and abortion that someone had thrust in his hand at the entrance, but that he had slid into his jacket pocket. He hung his vest on one of the coat hooks, feeling somewhat uncomfortable, as he always did in new surroundings.

Where am I going to sit? he wondered. *Not too far from the podium, so I can follow the lecture properly.*

He spied an empty seat next to an attractive woman. She glanced at him sideways. She had short, black hair that fell in strands before her dark eyes. She was slim and dressed stylishly in a black suit. Her pants were leather. He guessed her to be around thirty. He made sure his tie was straight.

ERESHKIGAL'S VENGEANCE

Should I take that empty seat next to her? What've I got to lose? Nothing, he thought. So he took his chances.

"Is this seat free?" he asked her.

"Sure, go ahead," she answered.

He sat down and placed his briefcase next to him. "My name is Gary Olson."

"I'm Barbro Berlind. Pleased to meet you."

With the ice now broken, he already felt more at ease. "Likewise. It's my first time here at Harvard. I still need to find my way around."

"It's familiar territory for me," Barbro said. "I studied here, did a doctorate, and am now doing further research at this university. I'm a pharmacologist. And you?"

"I work for the military as a virologist. So, we both conduct scientific research."

"You nurture the viruses in your lab as instruments; I find remedies for them."

"You're kidding, right? You're suggesting I make weapons out of them?"

He'd called her out. She raised her index finger to her pursed lips and gazed at him with her dark eyes. He found her quite sexy in that pose. "I don't nurture viruses to weaponize them," he responded. "I look for solutions in order to protect our troops and citizens. The army has ample resources for researching this at its disposal."

"The university's resources are rather limited. That means I can learn lots from you!" she said, flattering him. "That said, I think there's a very fine line between defensive and offensive weapons research. How, for instance, do you go about searching for cures for new viruses, created by people? Is there a huge temptation to also utilize those new viruses as biological weapons?"

"That temptation is certainly there, Barbro. It's an ethical question. As scientists, we frequently have to choose between morality and power."

Gary and Barbro got on well together. She was sophisticated and articulate. She cracked jokes during the breaks. Over the next few days, they'd often sit together in the auditorium before lectures.

"Your name, Barbro Berlind, intrigues me," said Gary. "It points to foreign origins. Yet you don't have any accent. Where does your name come from?"

"You first," answered Barbro.

"My last name, Olson, means son of Ole or Olof. I have Scandinavian ancestors."

"What a coincidence. My grandparents also come from Scandinavia, from Sweden. *Barbro* derives from the Greek *barbaros*, meaning foreigner or stranger. *Berlind* is a contraction of *bero*, bear, and *lind*, linden tree."

"Great, you have two natural elements in your name: an animal and a plant. Nature fascinates me. I enjoy researching plants and animals, viruses in particular. The smallest life-forms we know of. Viruses see to transferring genes differently to normal genetic reproduction. They increase genetic diversity in nature. Nature fits together so neatly."

She retorted, "Nature is brutal. Look at the lion devouring its prey. Or the banyan tree choking its host. Or the Ebola virus killing people."

"The lions and their prey, and the banyans and their hosts, are the ecosystem in equilibrium," Gary said. "A surplus of the one is corrected by the other. There's nothing wrong with that. The Ebola virus, on the other hand, broke out because humans had disrupted the jungle's ecosystem. You should never provoke viruses. You can, however, study them."

She helped him get his bearings of Harvard's university buildings. She told him, "I'd love to get a parking space in the BLS building, but they won't let me. Only VIPs are given a space."

⚬⚬⚬

As the course progressed, they increasingly confided in each other. Barbro handed Gary a few written sheets of paper and said,

"You couldn't take notes yesterday because your pen had run out. Here are copies of the ones I made."

"Thanks, Barbro. I really appreciate that a lot. I looked up some information for you on the vaccination against retroviruses."

"We're such a team!"

To his astonishment, Gary fell in love with her. He'd thought that was no longer possible. Might Barbro finally be a different type of woman than those he usually fell for? He held a spark of hope and meticulously copied her contact details from the course participants list. He asked her what her hobbies were.

"In my free time, I spend hours on improvisation-technique courses, to be able to think up something on the spot when I need to answer a question right away. I crave challenges. I aim to break my boundaries and overcome obstacles. I'd love to try parachute jumping, for instance. Another example is, I don't want GPS in my car because I want to find the way myself. I want to exercise and train my brain the way I like. The brain is such a powerful and marvelous thing."

"Just imagine if we could connect our brains together like in a computer network," he suggested.

"Between us, we'd be making creative-idea fireworks," she responded. "The possibilities would be endless. Besides my research position here at Harvard, I sometimes also work as a consultant for pharmaceutical companies. That pays well. With a multiple brain, we could achieve so much and make heaps of dough."

"Are you single?" Gary asked.

"I'm afraid so."

"How's that possible? You're pretty *and* you're nice."

Inside, she laughed. "Ha-ha. Yes, it's odd, isn't it? Men fear commitment, and more so with intelligent and confident women. My private life is a mess, but I'm a great networker. I'm like a chameleon. I adapt to whomever I'm talking to. I seize opportunities. In the street or when traveling, I'll talk to random people on the spur of the moment. I fall for men with a passion for something."

"Maybe we could go on a date," he suggested.

"You sure you dare?" she answered.

"Are you maybe a dominant? You always wear leather pants," he noted.

"I have a really short miniskirt too." She gave him a teasing smile.

"That's for special occasions!" he blushed. "When I was young, that would have seduced me. Now I look at personality more. Getting older means getting wiser. In my youth, I was so naive. In my teens, I'd keep falling down and getting up again."

"I have childhood traumas. I often used to make up stories and lie to my family and friends until my friends said, 'Barbro, what's actually true anymore?' That's when I stopped."

"Proper friends are important. I hardly have any friends and family. I have a daughter from a failed marriage. Her name's Sarah, and she means the world to me. She lives in Boston, and I'm visiting her this afternoon."

There was to be an exam on the last day of the course. Those who passed would receive a certificate. The course content was quickly summarized the day before. To prepare for this exam, the lecturer asked participants a number of questions that they had to answer as best they could.

"What is the antiviral effect of amantadine?" the course instructor asked.

Barbro answered. "It impedes the virus from entering the host cell."

"Absolutely right!"

"One down! Barbro, just how do you do it?" she remarked with triumph.

On the last day of the course, during lunch, Barbro suddenly confided in him. "I'm a serial killer." She smiled.

Gary was shocked. "What does that mean, Barbro?"

"I collect former coworkers and lovers."

Gary understood from this that, like a predator, she devoured one lover after another. He sensed danger, realizing that Barbro, just like those other women he'd fallen for in the past, was friendly and seductive on the outside, but ruthless on the inside. When he was still an adolescent, he was already drawn to the wrong kind of women: girls who seemed normal and who appeared perfectly nice and obliging, but who were in fact manipulative and unscrupulous in how they treated him. They had him worshiping them, in the palms of their hands, until they'd had enough of him and dumped him, brutally and unceremoniously. That had led him to despair. This despair would later turn to embitterment concerning women. The fact that his wife had left him for another man had only reinforced this view. Barbro was no better than those other women. He needed to be on his guard with her. Nevertheless, has was smitten and couldn't just ignore her now.

The exam was over. The course was at an end. Everyone went home. When it was time to say goodbye, Barbro looked Gary straight in the eyes with longing, as if asking for more. Gary thought to himself, *Watch out, Gary; don't fall into the trap. Control yourself.* He kissed her cheek. "I'll call you," he said. Without looking back, they went their separate ways.

Gary's reasoning commended him for managing to escape Barbro's clutches. Nonetheless, his feelings of love were clouding his senses. Shouldn't he have just tried starting something with her anyway?

———— ❤️ ————

Three months later. The Russian Academy of Science's research center in Pushchino, sixty miles south of Moscow.

The massive buildings stretched out along a green park over a mile in length. This center had a unique status and significance. It housed a substantial portion of the Russian Federation's endeavors in the field of physics, chemistry, and biomolecular biology. It employed over three thousand people, eight hundred of them holding doctorates in science or medicine. Pushchino scientists had made groundbreaking contributions to molecular and cell biology, bioorganic chemistry, plant and soil biology, as well as astronomy and astrophysics.

In the security-level 4 biological laboratory, Doctor Arkady Sokolov delicately placed several tubes of microorganisms into a transport case and sealed it, watertight and airtight, with the utmost care. He then placed the case into a decontamination lock.

He subsequently decontaminated himself in the chemical shower, then went to a room where he removed his pressure suit, and lastly, took a normal shower. After that, he went to the office of his boss, the somewhat older and paternalistic Doctor Ivan Kuznetsov.

"Hello, Ivan. Can I come in?" he asked.

"Of course, Arkady!"

"I'm on two weeks leave starting tomorrow. You approved this a while ago. I just came to say goodbye."

"Oh, yes. I remember now. Going away someplace?"

"Yes. Sochi, by the Black Sea."

"Ah, Sochi; the Russian Riviera! Arkady, my boy, you'll have a splendid time enjoying the sun and sea, the nature, the Caucus Mountains …"

"That's right, Ivan. Two weeks for me just to relax."

"And who knows? Maybe you'll find the love of your life there!"

"Maybe, but I came to ask you something. Before I go on to leave, I'd like to transfer a case of nonhazardous samples to Obolensk. I already completed the dispatch papers. Could you sign these, please?"

"Oh, Arkady, your dedication never ends! Let's see. It all seems in order."

Ivan signed the papers and handed them back to Arkady. "Well, then, I hope you enjoy your leave!"

"Thank you, Ivan. See you in two weeks!"

At the exit door, Arkady showed the security agent the completed and signed dispatch papers. On these, the guard read,

"Microorganisms, risk class 1. Accredited as a nonpathogen. Intended for the medical laboratory in Obolensk." He nodded his approval.

Arkady took a relieved breath, walked to his car with the case, and drove to the M2 Moscow-Leninskij freeway. However, once on the M2, he turned left toward Leninskij, rather than right toward Obolensk.

After around twelve miles, he took an exit near the village of Zaokskiy. He then drove onto a dead-end street. He parked in front of his house, opened the door, and entered with the case.

After a solitary dinner, he began packing his suitcases. He then went to bed early.

—∞∞∞—

The next morning, Arkady ate breakfast, double-checked he hadn't forgotten anything, and went to his car.

He placed the case and the luggage in the trunk, sat down behind the wheel, and drove off.

Arkady drove down the M2 once again, this time, southward. This continued for almost five hundred miles, with short breaks here and there, past Tula, Jelets, Voronez, and Pavlovsk, until he arrived in Millerovo, a city fifteen kilometers east of Ukraine— halfway to his destination. He stayed the night in the large-but-simple Hotel Druzhba. The following day, he continued driving south for around four hundred and eighty miles, past Kamensk-Shakhtinsky, Shakhty, Rostov-on-Don, Krasnodar, Tuapse, and finally on to Sochi. Sochi was a major city on the Black Sea, known for the 2014 Winter Olympics. It was also popular among Russians as a bathing resort and winter sports destination. Although the city's visitors were predominantly Russian, holding the Winter Olympics meant the city had now started attracting more foreign tourists. It was summertime, the period when tourists came to the city the most. This was when the climate was extremely pleasant, with temperatures around 70 °F and highs in the mid-80s.

Arkady was weary from the long journey and happy to find his downtown hotel: the five-star Hyatt Regency Sochi. This luxury establishment had a prime location by the coastline, right next to the famous Primorskaya Street seafront, and was just minutes away from the city's major cultural and leisure facilities, the passenger port, restaurants, high-end boutiques, nightclubs, and other attractions. Sochi International Airport was a mere twelve miles away, making the Hyatt Regency Sochi an excellent choice for business travelers and vacationers alike.

After a refreshing night's rest, Arkady dressed tourist-style, took breakfast, and returned to his room. He sent his room number to his contact, Mike, by WhatsApp. Fifteen minutes later, there was a knock on the door. He opened and saw a man wearing sunglasses and a flowery shirt.

"Doctor Sokolov?" asked the man.

"That's me."

"My name is Mike. Do you have the case?"

"Here it is."

"Perfect. Would you please follow me?"

Arkady grabbed the case and his luggage and followed the man.

"You can give me the case," said Mike.

"Be careful with it!"

"Rest assured, Doctor Sokolov. I'll take the greatest of care. Did everything go as planned?"

"Sure, I've taken two weeks leave from work. Not being there won't make anyone suspicious."

"Excellent! So, then, let's go fish!"

They strolled out of the hotel toward the Grand Marina, just a five-minute walk away. There, with the case and luggage, they boarded a small motorboat and sailed into the Black Sea.

"See this?" said Mike, "it's a GPS. With this, we can work

out exactly where we're sailing to. I'll set the destination to 43° 34′ north, and 39° 41′ east, which is just over two miles from Sochi."

After sailing for just over an hour, they arrived at the location entered. It wasn't long before an American submarine suddenly surfaced. Mike moored onto the submarine, right by the stepladder. Sailors from the US Navy appeared from the vessel and helped get Arkady, his case, and luggage aboard. The submarine then gracefully disappeared back beneath the water. Mike sailed back to Sochi.

Fifteen minutes later, Arkady met the captain of the vessel. "Welcome aboard the USS *John Warner*, Doctor Sokolov!"

"Thank you, Captain; I'm relieved everything went so smoothly."

"We're not there yet! We first have to leave the Black Sea undetected through the Bosporus, the Sea of Marmara, and the Dardanelles."

"Should I be concerned?"

"No, the USS *John Warner* is a state-of-the-art Virginia-class submarine. This means the vessel is silent, thanks to its pump–jet propulsion system. This makes it highly unlikely the Russians will notice us. You're in safe hands."

Sure enough, the submarine reached the Mediterranean without incident. Once there, the captain contacted the aircraft carrier USS *Abraham Lincoln*, and surfaced close by it. A Sikorsky SH-60 Seahawk helicopter swooped over from the carrier and hovered directly above the submarine, with a winch dangling down. Sailors helped Arkady into a harness and secured the winch to hoist him up to the chopper, as ever, with case and luggage in tow. The helicopter then dropped Arkady and the baggage off onto the aircraft carrier.

Arkady would not be aboard the carrier for long. A Grumman C-2 Greyhound flew him to the Aviano Air Base in Italy, but this was not his final destination either. A Boeing C-135 Stratolifter transport aircraft was ready and waiting. This took him to RAF Mildenhall in England, which also turned out to be just a stop-over. The C-135 finally crossed the Atlantic Ocean to the United

States and landed at the Andrews Air Force Base in Maryland. There, Arkady was given lodgings in comfortable officers' quarters.

A day later, a soldier arrived and escorted Arkady to the American Army's Medical Research Institute of Infectious Diseases (USAMRIID). This was the army's most important facility for defensive research into countermeasures against biological warfare. Located in Fort Derick, Maryland, it was the single laboratory of the American Ministry of Defense, equipped for studying extremely hazardous, biosafety level-four viruses in pressure suits. The USAMRIID engaged both military and civilian scientists, as well as specialized support personnel, around eight hundred people in total. Arkady Sokolov was met by one of those scientists: Gary Olson.

"Hello, Doctor Sokolov. Welcome to the USAMRIID. My name is Gary Olson, but please call me Gary! How was your journey here?"

"Very exciting, Gary. It was like a spy movie. I was in a submarine, on an aircraft carrier, and in a military transport plane. I am so happy it was a success. I am still accustoming myself to Western culture. The importance of personal space, the friendly people, the hamburgers …"

"Ha-ha-ha. I'm sure you'll get there. What do you drink: water, coffee, or soda?"

"Soda, please."

"Here, please take a seat. We have a great deal to discuss! So, you were working on a bioweapons program?"

"Yes, Russia's Biological Shield, that is its name. The president launched this eight years ago, contrary to the Biological Weapons Convention, which prohibits armaments of this nature. I could no longer live with the thought of immoral politicians potentially using these offensively. Look at the poisoning of Russian dissident Alexander Litvinenko with radioactive polonium in 2006, or the Novichok nerve gas assault on former Russian spy Sergei Skripal in 2018. Politicians preparing to do things such as these can likewise use biological weapons. This is why I defected to the West."

"And what's more, you brought along a case from the lab."

"I was able to smuggle this out because, allegedly, it contained only innocent microorganisms. In reality, these are extremely hazardous pathogens."

"Tell me more!"

"The first vial contains genetically modified anthrax, which is resistant to antibiotics and vaccination."

"That's a huge asset. Thanks to this sample, we'll be able to conduct research into antibodies against this form of anthrax, allowing us to prepare for a potential biological attack from Russia. And the second vial?"

"That contains a virus causing infertility in humans."

"How in the hell did you come up with that?"

"An intriguing story. Due to the global warming, Russia's tundra slowly started to thaw. As a result, animals from the distant past that had been frozen in the ice appeared on the surface. Our scientists seized this opportunity to study these animals. Because they possibly contained pathogens from long ago, against which humans might now lack resistance, these scientists worked with the utmost caution. And they indeed found a virus. Experiments on mice, monkeys, and humans indicated that this virus could be transmitted from animal to human, and from human to human, and that this caused infertility in women."

"Experiments on humans? How was that done?"

"It was conducted on those who were sentenced to execution and who had nothing more to lose."

"I see. And how does infertility arise?"

"The virus stimulates the creation of thyroid antibodies in humans, inducing fetus miscarriage at an early stage. Animals were vectors of the virus but remained asymptomatic and therefore fertile."

"When does this virus date from?"

"The virus was in live animals in the period between 3300 and 3200 BC, according to the carbon-14 dating method."

"Does a remedy for the virus already exist?"

"I know one medicine that has a temporary effect. I hope to collaborate with you in finding a permanent cure."

"Please, Doctor Sokolov. Your knowledge and expertise will be so very useful to us."

Gary Olson was an ardent proponent of ecocentrism, a philosophy in which nature, and not humanity, is central. He wanted to give nature back to nature. To this end, Gary concocted a plan to have the virus spread among people, thereby taking away women's fertility. Although he was no misogynist, he was disillusioned with women and with the way they'd treated him. He was willing to spread the virus causing female infertility without any scruples, as a form of retribution. The fact that humanity would therefore, in the long term, cease to exist was of little concern. Gary was known as a lone wolf: not confiding his intentions to a single soul. This meant there was no one to calm him down, to make him realize that only certain people were behind destroying the planet and that humanity as a whole did not deserve punishment. To bring his plan to fruition, Gary got in touch with Barbro Berlind. He called her.

"Hello, Barbro, it's Gary Olson. How are things?"

"Hey, Gary, what a pleasant surprise. Things are going great. I've often thought about you since the course we took together. Why are you calling?"

"Well, Barbro, I need you to help with a delicate venture that I'd like to discuss with you. Where and when could we meet? Preferably somewhere discreet, where we won't be disturbed."

"Hmm … this sounds exciting, Gary. I'm just dying to know more! We can meet at my place. Wednesday evening, I'm free after seven."

"Wednesday evening at eight is perfect. What's the address?" Gary asked.

Gary arrived right on time. He parked opposite Barbro's house. This turned out to be a small-yet-charming single-story house that, judging from the style, dated from the 1920s. He went up the steps and rang the bell. Barbro opened the door. She was dressed even more beautifully than she had been during their course. She wore a close-fitting black dress, and her slender legs were shrouded in alluring fishnet stockings with a lace top.

"Hi, Barbro!"

"Hi, Gary!"

He leaned in to kiss her cheek, but she turned her head so that the kiss landed on her sensual mouth.

"I've brought along this bottle of red wine," Gary said, holding it up.

"How thoughtful of you. You're such a sweetie," she answered. She showed him into the house.

"What an inviting living room!" Gary remarked.

"I put lots of effort into getting it right. Take a seat, Gary, and tell me about your plan!"

Barbro opened the bottle of wine and filled two glasses. They first got the small talk out of the way.

"Is that Shostakovich's "The Second Waltz" I can hear playing?"

"Yes. A magnificent waltz, isn't it?"

"A Viennese waltz composed by a Russian. Oh, this reminds me of the dance classes I used to take."

"I'm afraid I don't know that much about dancing, but there are plenty of other composers I love—Wagner, Holst, Mahler, Beethoven, Mozart, Bruckner, Berlioz, Stravinsky, and their dramatic repertoires in particular."

"Your taste in music is as great as your eyes are dark."

"Thank you. That's a nice compliment."

After ascertaining that they were alone in the house, Gary proceeded.

"Barbro, I'll get down to the point. I have a virus extracted from animals frozen in the tundra. It causes women to become infertile, but I can also provide a cure. Just imagine the virus spreading among the population. Whoever provides the cure would rake in phenomenal profits!" He paused a moment to observe her reaction.

Barbro sat forward on the edge of her chair. "Interesting. How would the virus be spread?"

"I've already thought of that, sweetheart," he answered confidently. "The virus survives a few weeks in water and can easily be dispersed using a vaporizer. All you need to do is send a bottle of perfume with the virus to dozens of unsuspecting people around the world. They could infect themselves. The virus is highly infectious and is transferred just like a cold, airborne, through coughing or sneezing, or by skin-to-skin contact, like through shaking hands. That way, people keep infecting others. A true epidemic could break out before anyone even realizes, given that infertility wouldn't be established immediately, but rather only after a few months or years."

"Why are you telling me this, Gary? What's the role for me that you have in mind?"

Gary sensed she'd taken the bait. She was every bit as money-grubbing as he'd thought. "That's simple, honey. You're a pharmacologist. Your contacts in the pharmaceutical world mean you can easily get the required number of perfume bottles manufactured and sent out to people as samples, promoting a new fragrance. Once the epidemic is in full swing, you can come forward with the cure and have it produced and sold by a pharmaceutical company you're a consultant for. We then both share the profits. I propose half and half. What do you think?"

Barbro thought about it and then said, "Are you positive no one will be able to track down the source of the virus or the bottles?"

"Absolutely positive," Gary answered. "After a few weeks,

the virus will have died in the bottles and will no longer be traceable long before anyone would start suspecting the bottles had something to do with the epidemic. By the way, it would be best to send out the bottles in the name of a fictitious company so nobody can find out we're behind it. Can I count on your collaboration, Barbro?"

Barbro's mind was at rest. "In this case, you can count on me, Gary. We're a team. I'll take care of spreading your virus, and afterward, distributing your remedy. And we get the revenue!"

They raised a toast to their venture being a success.

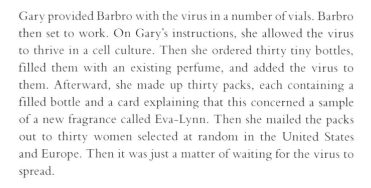

Gary provided Barbro with the virus in a number of vials. Barbro then set to work. On Gary's instructions, she allowed the virus to thrive in a cell culture. Then she ordered thirty tiny bottles, filled them with an existing perfume, and added the virus to them. Afterward, she made up thirty packs, each containing a filled bottle and a card explaining that this concerned a sample of a new fragrance called Eva-Lynn. Then she mailed the packs out to thirty women selected at random in the United States and Europe. Then it was just a matter of waiting for the virus to spread.

Gary called Barbro.

"Hey, Barbro, it's Gary. Have you got a minute?"

"Hey, Gary. Sure. Got any news?"

"Well, I have something to confess. The cure I have against the virus you spread—it only has a short-term effect on the people infected."

"You mean the cure stops the virus only temporarily?"

"That's right. Trials revealed that the medicine suppresses the virus for only a few weeks. After that, the disease once again appears, and the medicine no longer has any effect."

"You've let me down big time, Gary. Why did you have me spread the virus?"

"You know how I love nature, Barbro. Over time, I'd like humans to become extinct so nature can once again take control. It's humans who are responsible for everything that's going wrong in the world."

"Gary, now I'm furious with you. You deceived me and used me to spread the virus for your crackpot ideas."

"That's right, but now I know I was wrong. I found out yesterday that my daughter, Sarah, tried taking her life because she was diagnosed as infertile. It all points to her being infected by the virus. That opened my eyes. I'd like us both to look for a remedy together to cure my daughter. If we find a medicine that really works, you can still cash in on the earnings I promised from curing the people infected."

"You've sure got some nerve. I need to think about this. Call me back tomorrow."

Gary called Barbro again the next day.

"Hey, Barbro, it's Gary. Have you considered my proposal?"

"I have, Gary. I'm still furious with you, but I agree to collaborate with you to find a cure. We need to rectify this disaster that we've brought about. However, I have a few strict conditions.

"First, you must send me the virus again because I don't have any left. Out of precaution, I destroyed it last year so as not to leave any traces."

"Okay," Gary agreed. "And second?"

"You will also send me a description of the virus with as much information as possible about the DNA/RNA and a capsule of it."

"I'll do that. What else?"

"You will send me the explanation of the virus's origin. What's more, send me the placebo remedy. That might also still be useful. Send me all this without any further text or explanations. No emotions. If you do not comply, I'm not cooperating."

"I'll send everything exactly how you asked," Gary assured her.

"Lastly, I want to be sure that the two of us remain the only ones who know about my complicity in spreading the virus and searching for a remedy. In your remorseful frame of mind, you might just start talking to other people."

"I promise not to start talking."

"That's not enough. If you start talking, I'll get arrested. Now, listen carefully. I have a brother. He really dotes on me. He wouldn't be able to stand it if something happened to me. If that were the case, he'd take immediate action. He'll get to work on your daughter, Sarah. He works in a slaughterhouse, so you get my drift. This is what happened to an ex of mine. He now sleeps with the fishes."

"Why are you threatening me, Barbro? I just don't get it. Our secret is safe with me."

"I want to be able to rely on you, Gary—now and in the future. That's why I've got my brother in reserve. He's my insurance for your silence."

"As you wish, but that won't be necessary. You can count on it."

"Whatever happens?" she asked.

"Whatever happens," he promised.

"We need to find a plausible explanation for our phone calls, in case you get taken in."

"What do you want me to say in that case?"

"I think you should say only that you proposed that we jointly find a cure for the virus you discovered, but that I didn't want to collaborate. Is that clear, Gary?"

"Crystal clear!"

CHAPTER 5

ix months later, the pandemic first started appearing in the press. Despite her dealings with Gary, Barbro still had found no cure for the disease with a permanent effect, and desperation was setting in. She thought she'd have a greater chance of finding a remedy if she were collaborating with the authorities than working with Gary. Barbro decided to get in touch with her former PhD supervisor, Steve Patters, who was now one of the directors of the CDC, and provide partial information. She hoped to come up with a cure through the CDC and have it produced by Farmoso, a pharmaceutical company she was a consultant for.

Barbro looked up Steve Patters's phone number and tapped it into her cell phone.

"Hello, Steve here."

"Hey, Steve. It's Barbro Berlind."

"Hey, Barbro, it's been quite a while! How are things with you?"

"Great, thanks. And with you?"

"Things are going great. But public health leaves a lot to be desired. Did you read our press release?"

"Yes, I did. That's actually the reason I called. I have significant new information on the infertility epidemic."

"Tell me!"

"Six months ago, I was contacted by a certain Gary Olson, a military virologist. I'd met this man previously during a class, and he fell in love with me. He told me he'd discovered a virus in frozen animals dug up from the Russian tundra. He'd performed tests with that virus and established that it caused infertility in women. He spread that virus among people out of some bizarre notion that humanity would be better off dying out, to benefit nature. Afterward, when his daughter turned out infertile, he saw the error of his ways. He asked me if, together, based on the virus and a cure with a temporary effect, we could develop a cure that works permanently. I didn't think this was serious, and I didn't take him up on his offer. This morning, I read the press release announcing an infertility epidemic. It started dawning on me that there was something much more severe going on here than I'd at first realized. I thought I had to notify the CDC of this information."

"You did a good thing, Barbro. Thank you! Your information provides us insight into the origin of this disease and might just lead to a breakthrough in resolving the epidemic."

"I'm prepared to give my full cooperation in this as a pharmacologist."

"Excellent! I'll notify my colleague Shira Fox, the epidemiologist in charge of this case, right away. Your cooperation is highly appreciated. I'll keep you updated on the latest developments."

After the call with Barbro, Steve rushed over to Shira's office.

"Hey, Shira, I'm glad you're in! I have new information about the epidemic!"

Steve told her what he'd learned from Barbro. "So, now you know as much as I do."

"Can this Barbro be trusted?" Shira asked.

"Absolutely. I used to teach Barbro at Harvard Medical School. She went on to get a doctorate in pharmacology. I was her tutor. I remember Barbro as an outstanding student and a hard and dedicated worker who always got results.

"What do we do about that Gary Olson?"

"I see no other choice but to inform the FBI right away so they can question him."

Based on this information, Gary was arrested. Ecocentric literature was discovered in his computer. Following the arrest, the Department of Defense saw itself obliged to collaborate in the investigation. Samples of the virus were found in the military laboratory where Gary had worked. Officials compared the DNA of those laboratory viruses with the DNA of the infertility virus in infected people and proved that the global pandemic was indeed based on one of those lab viruses. This corroborated Barbro's story, meaning they believed her story.

Despite admitting his guilt, Gary didn't confess about Barbro because of his fear of retaliation against his daughter Sarah. Arkady Sokolov confessed to having smuggled the infertility virus with him from Russia during his defection to the West, and that he'd taken Gary into his confidence but regretted it terribly. Arkady was also able to say that the animals, dug up from the tundra, dated from the period between 3300 and 3200 BC, according to the carbon-14 dating method.

The media pounced on this story, with headlines such as: "Danger from the Tundra, Bioweapon Basis of Pandemic, Virologist Confesses" and "Russian Virus on the Loose."

CNN devoted an entire broadcast to the use of biological weapons:

"And now we're talking live with Doctor Eddie Lewis, who works at Xavier University in Cincinnati, Ohio. Doctor Lewis, what do we mean by biological weapons?" the newscaster said.

"Biological weapons comprise all microorganisms—like bacteria, viruses, or fungi, or toxins, poisonous substances produced by microorganisms—that are found in nature and that can be used to kill or harm people," Dr. Lewis said.

"So, a kind of bioterrorism?" the newscaster asked.

"That's right. The terrorist act might vary from a simple

threat to actually using these biological weapons, also known as agents. Certain nations have or are attempting to acquire biological tools of war, and there are major concerns that terrorist groups or individuals might obtain the technologies and expertise to use these destructive substances. Biological agents can be used for an isolated assassination as well as to cause thousands of people to be incapacitated or killed. Once the environment has been contaminated, this can create a protracted threat to the population."

"How many of these agents are there, and how easy is it to use them as weapons?"

"Despite there being more than twelve hundred biological agents that can be used to cause disease or death, relatively few possess the features required to make them ideal candidates for biological warfare or terrorist activities. Acquiring, processing, and using the ideal biological weapons is fairly straightforward. Only small quantities—in the order of kilograms and often less—would be needed to kill or to eliminate hundreds of thousands of people in metropolitan areas. Biological weapons are easy to conceal, and it's hard to detect or protect yourself against them. They're invisible, odorless, tasteless, and can be spread silently."

"When were bioweapons first used?"

"Using biological agents isn't anything new, and history's full of examples of their application. Attempts to use biological weapons date back to ancient times. Scythian archers were already infecting their arrows in 400 BC by dipping them into decomposing corpses or in blood blended with dung. Persian, Greek, and Roman literature from 300 BC cites examples of dead animals being used to poison wells and other water sources.

"In the battle of the Eurymedon in 190 BC, Hannibal won a maritime victory over King Eumenes II of Pergamon by flinging clay casks full of venomous snakes onto the enemy ships," Dr. Lewis explained.

"Quite remarkable. It's giving me cold shivers."

"During the battle of Tortona in the AD twelfth century, Barbarossa poisoned wells using the dead, decomposing bodies of soldiers. During the siege of the Port of Caffa in the AD fourteenth century, the attacking Tartar troops hurled plague-riddled corpses into the city in an attempt to cause an epidemic among enemy troops. This succeeded, and the Genovese merchants present—both healthy and sick—fled back to Europe by boat. This gave rise to an unforeseen catastrophe: the plague quickly spread throughout the continent, and twenty-five million people—over a quarter of Europe's population—perished."

"Horrific!"

"The method was repeated in 1710, when the Russians besieging Swedish troops in Reval catapulted bodies of people who'd died of the plague. That tactic worked. Plague broke out within the walls of Reval. However, the dying population had no way to escape, and the epidemic was confined to the city."

"Are there also examples from the Americas?"

"In the eighteenth century, the British were fighting the French and its Indigenous allies for domination of what would become Canada, during the French and Indigenous wars. The British saw to the Indigenous people acquiring sheets infected with smallpox. This decimated them, since they'd never previously been exposed to the disease and had no immunity."

"That's terrible. A real genocide. But we know, in particular, about splenic fever—also called anthrax—as a bioweapon. Could you tell me a bit more about that?"

"The first time anthrax was used as a weapon was during the First World War. At that time, Scandinavian rebels used the bacteria in Finland against the Russian army in 1916. There's also evidence that the Germans used anthrax to infect the enemy's cattle. After the war, biological warfare such as this was banned by the Geneva Protocol, but this treaty wasn't honored since no method of verification existed there."

"How did that work out?"

"In the 1930s, the Japanese experimented with virtually every hazardous virus and bacterium known at the time, such as anthrax, cholera, bubonic plague, salmonella, typhoid, tetanus, brucellosis, botulism, gangrene, malaria, smallpox, meningococcus meningitis, tuberculosis, tularemia, and glanders. Tests were conducted on animals, but also on prisoners of war. Following this test phase, they proceeded to attack eleven Chinese cities. In this assault, they spread various diseases over houses from an aircraft with the intention of causing epidemics."

"Gruesome! The Second World War broke out shortly after."

"The United States and Great Britain then started large-scale experiments with biological weapons. The United States filled more than five thousand bombs with anthrax 'just in case.' Britain held exercises with anthrax bombs on flocks of sheep on Gruinard Island off Scotland. A significant finding of Britain's experiments was that anthrax remains in the environment for a very long time. Gruinard was inaccessible until 1986, when the government decided to decontaminate the entire island."

"I didn't know about that."

"And there's more. From 1940 to 1956, the Canadian government conducted experiments with anthrax and rinderpest on Grosse Île, an island on the St. Lawrence River in Quebec Province. The allies used these to ready themselves for a bacteriological war against Nazi Germany. No less than four hundred thirty-nine liters of anthrax were produced, the equivalent of seventy billion fatal doses."

"Enough to wipe out the total world population ten times over. That's shocking!"

"Quite. During the 1970s, there was growing international pressure to bring about a ban on biological weapons. In 1968, Great Britain proposed that a disarmament be signed, and the Warsaw Pact members also raised pressure. In 1969, President Nixon halted the biological weapons program and destroyed the stocks. From then on, the only thing the United States was occupied with was preventing and combating such infectious diseases."

"What happened after that?"

"A number of countries pursued offensive research into using biological weapons. What's more, terrorist organizations have become users of biological agents since the 1980s."

"Tell us some more!"

"It's supposed that in London, in 1978, a dissident Bulgarian journalist, Georgi Markov, was assassinated by order of Bulgaria's secret service by stabbing him with an umbrella tip, embedding a minuscule, spherical steel pellet into the muscle fiber. The pellet was perforated and had space for around 0.3 milligrams of toxin. Markov died a couple of days later. Based on the symptoms and the minimal quantity of poison that could be used, it's accepted this must have been ricin. There's no direct evidence."

"There was also a threat from Iraq …"

"Right. In 1985, Iraq commenced an offensive biological weapons program producing anthrax, botulinum toxin, and aflatoxin. During Operation Desert Storm, the coalition of allied troops was confronted with the threat of chemical and biological agents. After the Persian Gulf War, it was discovered that Iraq had bombs, Scud missiles, 122 mm missiles, and artillery grenades armed with botulinum, anthrax, and aflatoxin. They also had spray tanks in aircrafts that could spread those agents over a specific target."

"Bulgaria and Iraq are countries. Can you provide some examples of terrorist organizations?"

"Sure. In September and October 1984, seven hundred and fifty-one people were deliberately infected with salmonella, which causes food poisoning, when followers of the Bhagwan Shree Rajneesh contaminated restaurants in Oregon. In 1994, a Japanese sect of the Aum Shinrikyo cult sprayed an anthrax aerosol from the tops of buildings in Tokyo.

"In 1995, two members of a militia group in Minnesota were convicted of possessing ricin, which they had produced themselves to use as a retribution against local government officials. Fear arose once again when, in 2001, in the aftermath of the terrorist attack of September 11, letters with powder were discovered. On September 18 and October 9, 2001, four letters containing powders were encountered, two to US senators and two to press agencies. The powder turned out to contain anthrax spores, and opening the letter meant the spores could spread in the air and be inhaled. This powder-letter attack was reported later, because it was only clear after a few days that people had been infected. Eleven people were contaminated through inhalation and eleven through skin contact. Five died, with all the victims being among those who'd breathed in the powder. After this attack, letters like this were monitored and checked, and the FBI commenced a thorough investigation into who sent the letters.

"After a seven-year investigation, the FBI pointed to the lab technician Bruce Edwards Ivins as the culprit in August 2008, without being able to prove his role in the affair. Ivins died of an overdose a few days prior to the FBI report."

"I remember that," the newscaster said. "The attack was known as Amerithrax."

"And there's more. In December 2002, six terrorist suspects were arrested in Manchester, England. Their apartment was being used as a ricin lab. Among them was a twenty-seven-year-old chemist who produced the toxin. Later, on January 5, 2003, the British police raided two homes in London and found ricin spores, leading to an investigation into a possible Chechen-separatist plan to attack the Russian Embassy with the toxin. Various arrests were made."

"It never ends …"

"Quite. In October 2003, a letter with ricin, signed 'Fallen Angel,' was discovered in a postal facility in Greenville, South Carolina. The letter demanded new 'hours of service' rules requiring more breaks for truck drivers be rescinded. A second ricin letter was sent to the White House in November 2003, containing comparable language and threatening to turn DC in a ghost town. Then, on February 3, 2004, a number of US Senate office buildings were evacuated after ricin was found in a mail room serving the office of Bill Frist, the Senate's majority leader. These three cases were linked to each other by investigators, although no arrests were ever made.

"Three letters with ricin were intercepted in April 2013, addressed to President Barack Obama, Senator Roger Wicker, and Judge Sadie Holland. In this case, the culprit was quickly apprehended and convicted. And that was the sad list of terrorist acts with biological weapons so far."

"And so now we have the infertility virus, released into the population by Gary Olson, an outlandish scientist. This has to be the worst-ever act in the history of biological warfare."

Ralph heard about his father-in-law Gary Olson's arrest on the radio. He called Sarah right away.

"Sarah?"

"Hi, Ralph."

"I've got bad news, honey. It was just on the radio. Your dad's been arrested."

"What? But why?"

"A virus causing infertility. He apparently spread it."

"But … that's impossible! I just can't believe it."

"Remember what he said about us wanting a baby?"

"Yeah."

"And that he'd prefer people to disappear instead of reproducing?"

"Yeah, those were his words …"

"So, it could well be he's behind the epidemic, couldn't it?"

"I'm in shock. Dad's the cause of my infertility …"

"As a virologist in the army, he had access to the most dangerous viruses."

"Oh, Ralph, I'd only just started getting over my depression, and now this. I just feel awful."

"I understand, honey. What a situation, huh? I'm coming straight over to be there for you."

When Ralph got home, he saw there was already another car parked outside the house. Would Sarah have visitors? He went in and found Sarah, in tears, with two unknown men.

"Ralph, these are FBI agents. They confirm that Dad's in custody."

"And now you want us to tell you what we know about Gary, right?" Ralph asked the two men.

"You could say that. But we also want to express our sympathies for you. It must be a real shock to find out your father or father-in-law is in jail."

"It sure is," Ralph said. "I just heard it on the radio."

"We came as soon as we could. Did you know anything about Gary's plans?"

"No, not at all. Gary's a fairly closed person and didn't talk about his work as a military virologist."

"There was no suspicion or indication whatsoever that he'd put a virus into circulation?"

"No. The only thing we knew was that he was against us trying for a baby, and that he put nature first, above people. It seemed pretty unusual. Maybe there's some motive for his actions in that."

"We think so too. Who are his friends?"

"Erm … I don't know any of Gary's friends. Sarah, do you know?"

"No, Ralph. Dad was a loner who lived for this work. He hasn't got any friends."

"Is he a member of any associations?"

"Not that I know of," Sarah said.

"Well, in that case, we have no more questions. If anything else comes to you that might be useful to the investigation, please let us know. Here's our card."

The FBI agents exited the house, leaving Sarah and Ralph behind, distraught. Ralph did his best to console Sarah with a long hug.

Scientists christened the virus the Human Fertilodeficiency Virus (HFV). Since it was now clear that this was a transmittable virus, additional measures needed to be taken to contain its spread until medication became available. The emergency plan was adjusted. Travel was still allowed only for work, shopping, health, and emergency situations. Any other journeys were prohibited. Flights were permitted only for essential travel. People had to take social spaces into account and keep a distance of at least five feet apart. A ban on gatherings meant that public life was severely restricted. All events with more than five participants were canceled. Wearing face masks on public transport became compulsory. The authorities asked banks to provide credit facilities for the sectors most affected, such as tourism, bars and restaurants, culture, and aviation. The bulk of the losses had to be absorbed by a credit package for the self-employed and companies hit by the crisis. Business and private individuals were also granted payment deferments from banks. The government also created a compensation fund, and, together with the central banks, created a stimulus package for the economy. Finally, a temporary unemployment system was put into action. People were advised to take the following preventative measures: washing hands regularly, coughing and sneezing into a handkerchief or on the inside of the elbow, avoiding handshakes, staying at home if sick, and avoiding nonessential travel. People with specific questions about what was and wasn't possible could visit websites with chat channels, where chatbots provided the answers.

Researchers and pharmacologists in medical laboratories all around the planet, Barbro Berlind among them, were feverishly searching for a vaccine or a remedy—unsuccessfully for the time being. They kept each other informed through videoconferencing. Meanwhile, as the months passed, the epidemic proliferated. In one of Shira Fox's video calls with other epidemiologists around the globe, it sounded alarming.

"I'm shocked," said Shira. "Recent random samples reveal

that three quarters of all people in the United States have already been infected."

"Here in Europe things aren't much better, said a WHO epidemiologist. "Blood tests of patients show us that half of all people here have the disease. Placing people in quarantine is a hopeless task."

"Our Alarm Code Orange disaster plan has delayed the epidemic somewhat, but it has by no means stopped it," Shira admitted. "That is highly disturbing. The medical labs are all working on finding a vaccine or a cure. Once we reach that point, we need to have a plan ready for containing the epidemic globally. Public-private cooperation will be required. We can already start negotiating partnerships, defining the nature and scope of the private sector's involvement in a transparent manner."

"Could you explain that some more, Shira?" someone asked.

"Sure. The expertise and services of various industries deserve special attention. The first is the pharmaceutical industry, which plays a key role in researching, developing, and producing medical countermeasures. The second is comprised of airlines, transportation, and logistics, which can handle transporting medical staff and equipment when upscaling operations.

"The third is the medical-supplies industry, which also has major global importance and can contribute toward researching, developing, and producing countermeasures. And a fourth is the worldwide communications sector. This encompasses both those supplying hardware and software concerning communication and those leading globally in delivering content and providing assistance for public information requirements.

"Medicine production will be a critical issue. Most of our medicine-production capacity involves a handful of pharmaceutical companies in only a few countries. These companies have optimized their production output based on expected demands for their products. That means there's little peak capacity in the system. Companies will be faced with getting commercial production off-line, and instead will manufacture medicines for the new disease.

"Manufacturers might also come under political pressure to produce medicines for their home countries before exporting these to the rest of the world. This might mean only a few countries have access to medication until production can be substantially expanded, which could take months or even years. Individual countries can purchase the required stocks and distribute this among their populations.

"That might still work out in developed countries such as the United States, European member states, Japan, China, and Russia. However, I'm worried about undeveloped countries. There, the availability, distribution, and administration of medicines can get ensnared because of a lack of capable authorities and health care structures. This poses the risk of lingering epidemic hotspots. In those cases, we'll have to call on international emergency funds and donations from philanthropic institutions or other organizations to finance the aid for these countries," Shira explained.

Since there was still no effective medicine, fake medicines appeared on the market. Certain influencers were promoting "spurgia" or "pronascia" on social media. Pharmacies were inundated with requests for these drugs. Shira knew she had to do something about this. She distributed a press release through the official media warning the public not to use these drugs, since they provided no proven effect whatsoever. However, this didn't sit well with the influencers. They posted comments such as, "The CDC is exaggerating the epidemic and is lying about medicines to gain more power for themselves." One follower even wrote, "There's a conspiracy happening. Shira Fox is deliberately withholding information. She's a nasty bitch and a manipulator."

Shira was infuriated. She sought out support from her boss, Steve Patters, and was allowed to use the CDC Facebook page to defend herself. She wrote:

"The CDC is hereby announcing that the current policy concerning the infertility epidemic and the HFV virus is based on the joint work of top scientists, including the CDC's head epidemiologist Shira Fox. The CDC prioritizes public health and is behind the approach recommended by its scientists. Taking fake drugs such as spurgia or pronascia, as sometimes recommended on social media, is absolutely pointless."

Adherents of the Wicca movement, who worshiped pagan gods, implored the Mother Goddess to end the infertility epidemic in rituals.

⸙

One day, Shira Fox received an entirely unexpected message from Professor Alexander Bullock in her mailbox.

> *Dear Shira,*
>
> *A recent excavation in Iraq has brought new clay tablets to light. I have just translated these, and this appears to be a new fragment of the story concerning Inanna and the infertility epidemic during the Sumerian civilization in Mesopotamia. In light of the global infertility epidemic currently raging unabated, I felt I ought to inform you of this as quickly as possible. The translation reads as follows:*
>
> *After the goddess Inanna had returned from the underworld unscathed, her high priests healed the people and the beasts with the remedy that Kurgarra and Galatur had received from Ereshkigal. The high priests recorded this remedy for the plague of barrenness on the Mes clay tablets so that this would be archived for posterity. However, Ereshkigal demanded that part of the Mes be kept in the underworld so that her power might be preserved. Once the epidemic had waned, in gratitude, the dwellers of Uruk erected a new stone temple called the House of Inanna and Ereshkigal above the tunnel with the seven gates to the*

underworld. This temple was adorned with exquisite reliefs of the divine pair, Inanna and Ereshkigal.

Kind regards,
Professor Alexander Bullock

Shira called Alexander right away. "Hello, Alexander. Thanks for sending the translation of the new fragment."

"My pleasure!" he said.

"This might be significant. When exactly does the infertility epidemic date to during the Sumerian civilization?"

"It ends with the construction of the House of Inanna and Ereshkigal in Uruk," Alexander answered. "The archaeologists who excavated the city of Uruk date the temple's construction to the late Uruk period, which is between 3400 and 3100 BC."

"This dating corresponds with the dating of the frozen animals from the tundra that had been infected with the Human Fertilodeficiency Virus," Shira noted. "That means the infertility epidemic currently affecting the world must have been caused by the same virus as that of the infertility epidemic during the late Uruk period of the Sumerian civilization."

"But how could the virus span such a long time and distance?"

"The virus was able to survive for more than five thousand years, dormant in the frozen animals of the Russian tundra. The infertility epidemic in the Inanna story appears to have extended beyond Sumer, throughout the entire Eurasian continent."

"That seems like a plausible explanation," Alexander opined. "The high priests wrote down the remedy on the Mes. That means to find the past and present cure, we need to unearth the Mes, which is still located in the underworld, under the House of Inanna and Ereshkigal in Uruk, since so far only the temple's superstructure has been excavated."

"Alexander, we've got a lead for finding the remedy! We need to notify the government of this right away!" Shira said.

Shira and Alexander informed the US government. Ron J. Adams, president of the United States of America, invited them to attend a meeting in the Oval Office, where they relayed their information. Also present were the national security advisor, the secretary of health and human services, and Stephen Alborough, the secretary of defense.

"If I understand right," said the president, "the cure for the epidemic has been written down on clay tablets that can be found under a certain temple in Uruk, in southern Iraq. So, we need to organize an emergency excavation under that temple."

"That is indeed our recommendation, Mr. President," said Shira. "The temple dates from the Sumerian period, predating the rise of Islam. That means the Iraqis won't have religious objections to an excavation."

"Once the clay tablets are found, I can translate these to ascertain the remedy," said Alexander. "Translating Sumerian cuneiform is my specialty."

The president thought for a moment. He wanted to take effective and principled action in the footsteps of his illustrious forefathers, the presidents John Adams and John Quincy Adams, the second and sixth presidents of the United Stated, respectively. He then remarked, "While Iraq might be an ally of ours, it's certainly not a safe country. There are religious fanatics over there who regularly carry out bombings, terrorist actions, and kidnappings. We'll have to have the excavation teams under military protection. I'll order both an archaeological and a military expedition. What do you think, Stephen?"

"That seems like a good plan, Mr. President," Stephen said. "To create as much goodwill as possible, and not come across as the Lone Ranger, I recommend enlisting the help of allied countries and acting jointly as a 'coalition of the willing.' That assistance can be of both an archaeological and a military nature. The United States will, of course, retain supreme command."

"An excellent suggestion, Stephen. I'll go right now to

the Situation Room to hold a videoconference with several heads of state and government leaders, asking them to provide assistance."

The president thus consulted with the leaders of Great Britain, France, Germany, China, and Iraq. Iraq had to be involved, since Uruk was within its territory. All the countries proved ready to join the coalition. The Iraqi leader also requested guarantees that his country's sovereignty would be safeguarded, and that the military operations be limited to what was essential for protecting the archaeological expedition. This was because Iraq's population had grown weary of war and averse to foreign interference following various invasions and the struggle against the Islamic State.

Shira and Alexander were assigned to assisting the Uruk excavation team. Alexander had cutting-edge equipment for scanning, reading, and translating the clay tablets. As a backup for Alexander, the young German archaeologist and clay-tablet translator Odo Holz would also join the excavation team.

Shira wanted one more pharmacologist for the team. She consulted with her boss, Steve Patters, on this.

"Hey, Steve, we still need another pharmacologist on the team going to Iraq. Do you know of anyone suitable?"

"Oh, Shira; if I were still young, I'd go along myself. But now, I'd rather leave that to someone else. I recommend Barbro Berlind. Her skills will be exactly what you need over there."

Prior to contacting Barbro, Shira examined the woman's LinkedIn profile online. She read through Barbro's résumé. There were also testimonials from various people: "Barbro is an extremely valuable member of our medical team. Not only is she an advanced pharmacologist, but she is also quickly developing expertise in the field of virology and bacteriology. She delivers this with sharpness and humor that keeps everyone on their toes. Working with her is a true pleasure."

Another recommendation read: "I've known Barbro for more than two years, and I can confirm that she is genuinely a terrific professional and a talented biomedic, with multidisciplinary skills. She followed the various research procedures meticulously, with a clear understanding of the objectives. Moreover, it was a real pleasure talking with her about these matters, owing to her communicative enthusiasm."

Another said: "Barbro Berlind was fantastic to work with. Not only did she guide me patiently through the labyrinth of human physiological processes, but she was also extremely pleasant to work with during both the early and late hours. I wouldn't hesitate one instance to work with her again."

The final one said: "As a pharmacologist, she acted as a consummate professional. Her positive attitude and readiness to help with a problem multiple times accelerated the progress of research assignments. Working with her was amazing. You can ask me for a reference about Barbro's qualities and skills directly, on paper, or by telephone."

Shira called Barbro and explained the goal of the expedition. "We'd like to add a pharmacologist to the team to help me out on-site with interpreting the clay tablets medically and to subsequently provide the pharmaceutical companies with correct information on the nature of the medicine they'll have to produce to cure humans and animals. I thought of you on account of your reputation as a researcher at Harvard and your contacts in the pharmaceutical world. What do you think? Are you prepared to join the team as a pharmacologist?"

"I most certainly am," Barbro said. "I love an adventure. I'm grateful that you thought of me. Being able to take part is a real honor. I'll give it all I've got; I can promise you that."

"Great. That's so good to hear. From now on, you're officially on the team. I'm looking forward to our collaboration!"

The latest developments were once again plastered all over the media: "Race for a Remedy: Wrath of the Goddess, the Temple of Cure" and "Iraq Invasion 3.0." The latter headline referred to the first invasion of Iraq, in 1991, to liberate Kuwait from the clutches of Saddam Hussein, and the second invasion of the country in 2003, when he was finally overthrown.

CHAPTER 6

The coalition troops occupied Uruk and the neighboring village of al-Khidhir in southern Iraq with military ostentation. Both a military camp and an excavation camp were set up close by. The coalition stationed a helicopter deck ship, the *USS Boxer*, in the Persian Gulf, from where it could provide the excavation team with air support and supply it with essential provisions and equipment. Given Iraq's lack of security, this remote support was no gratuitous luxury.

Shira, Alexander, and Barbro were flown on a Boeing C-135 Stratolifter transport aircraft from the United States to Bahrain in the Persian Gulf. Located here was the Naval Support Activity Bahrain, home base of the US Naval Forces Central Command and the Fifth Fleet. There, they were introduced to German archaeologist Odo Holz, who'd flown over from his home country.

"Welcome to the team, Odo," said Shira. "It promises to be a thrilling undertaking. Now that we're all together, I'd like to know your personal motivations behind taking part in the expedition. I'll get the ball rolling with mine. I'm passionate about bringing people together and about organizing. What's more, I defend standards and values that keep families and communities united. You can simply call me a manager. For as long as I can remember, this is how I wanted to make a difference, and I'll do all it takes to make that happen."

"My involvement is about inspiring others to do the right thing," said Alexander. "Moreover, I wish to preserve and promote our heritage—texts and clay tablets in particular."

"I'm in this for the adventure, despite the danger," Barbro admitted. "I sometimes even seek out risks. I get a kick out of it. Life would just be dull otherwise, right?"

"To me, it's a new project in which I can indulge my knowledge and skills in ancient languages," said Odo. "I really hope we'll find the clay tablets so that we can analyze them."

"Great," Shira noted. "With all these motivations, we'll be able to tackle any issue we encounter from a whole range of angles. We are a truly complementary team. Alexander, the inspirer; Barbro, the daredevil; Odo, the thinker; and me, the manager."

"That means our team has two leader figures," Barbro observed. "Shira, the great organizer, and Alexander, the charismatic leader. That might also mean the occasional clash."

"We've gotten along just fine so far, haven't we, Alexander?" asked Shira.

"We have, indeed, and let's keep it that way. Let's form a tight team, all reading from the same page. That's how we'll accomplish the most."

"While translating the tablets might lead to a touch of rivalry between Alexander and me, that's healthy competition," said Odo.

They left Bahrain on a V-22 Osprey tilt-rotor aircraft, escorted by Apache helicopters, to the *USS Boxer* for refueling. Then they flew on to the camps in Iraq. They landed in a heliport near Uruk, alighted, and were welcomed by the expedition's commandant.

"Hello, scientists; welcome to Iraq! I'm Colonel Stuart Mackay. Central Command informed me of your arrival."

"Hello, Colonel, a pleasure to meet you. I'm Shira, and these are my colleagues, Alexander, Barbro, and Odo. How are things here?"

"Excellent. You're in luck, weatherwise. It's March, and the daytime temperature is an agreeable 77 °F, and goes down to 60 °F at night. But just watch out for the sun. It can really scorch.

Applying sunscreen regularly and sheltering during peak heat hours is advised."

Colonel Mackay gave Shira, Alexander, Barbro, and Odo a guided tour of the two camps.

"As you can see, the excavation camp is close to the ruins of Uruk. The military camp is located right next to the excavation camp on the road between Uruk and the village of al-Khidhir to guarantee maximum security for the excavators and the scientists. There are several communal facilities situated halfway between both camps, such as the catering, the dining tent, the showers, the latrines, the fitness and relaxation area, the sickbay, the vehicle fleet, the heliport, the fuel supply, the power generators, the computer room, and the telecommunications equipment—including a satellite connection and a GSM mast."

"Is there Wi-Fi?" asked Barbro.

"Sure. Each tent is equipped with a Wi-Fi access point. Each camp also has its own sleeping tents. Most of these are shared. The soldiers have their sleeping tents in the military camp, and the excavators are in the excavation camp. But you four are getting the VIP treatment, as much as is possible in this desert. To allow you a degree of privacy, you each have your own separate tent in the excavation camp."

"What a luxury!" Alexander joked.

"What happens with the dirty laundry?" asked Shira.

"The Osprey flies the laundry over to the helicopter deck ship, where it's washed and ironed, and then flown back here."

After the tour, they explored the ruins of the ancient city of Uruk, accompanied by a local guide, Kadeem Awad, from al-Khidhir. Kadeem explained with enthusiasm, "The old Sumerian city of Uruk dates from 4000 BC. This was the largest city in Sumer, 5.5 square kilometers in surface area, with a city wall 19.5 kilometers long, and with a population of around fifty thousand inhabitants at its peak. Uruk was not just the largest agglomeration of the first urban civilization on Earth, but it is also the place where the first writing was discovered. The oldest dates from

3300 BC. The city was abandoned only around AD 450, probably because of a branch of the Euphrates silting up.

"However, they were particularly interested in what still remained of the temple of Inanna and Ereshkigal. That primarily turned out to be the foundation and a number of man-sized walls, broad columns, and steps."

Something rugged in the vicinity of the temple almost made Barbro trip up. Odo just managed to catch her.

"Thank you, Odo," she said. "You've got quick reflexes. I nearly fell over. But over what, exactly?"

"It seems to be a narrow crevice in the ground," he said.

"Quite! And that's not the only one," Barbro said.

"Could there be a connection between those crevices and the seven gates to the underworld?" Shira wondered aloud.

"There might well be!" Alexander agreed. "The seven gates to the underworld most likely refer to the subterranean passages and spaces under the House of Inanna and Ereshkigal."

"Kadeem," asked Shira, "can you tell us more about those crevices and what's underground?"

"Unfortunately not, miss; but the village elder, Farrah al-Rashid, would be able to. However, Farrah is currently at the hospital in Samawah, a city eighteen miles to the west of Uruk."

"Okay. Are you willing to accompany me to Samawah? You'll be paid generously for doing so."

"Of course! Kadeem is at your service."

"Great, thank you!"

———⊱⊰———

Shira went to Colonel Stuart Mackay. "Hello, Colonel."

"Hello, Shira, how are the preparations in the excavation camp going?"

"They're going well, thank you. I'm here to ask you a favor. I'd like to speak with the village elder, Farrah al-Rashid, about the crevices we came across in the ground surrounding the temple.

Farrah is currently in Samawah. Could I please be given a military escort to protect me for the trip to Samawah and back?"

"I can arrange that, but I'd like to emphasize that you take the utmost caution. Foreigners are frequently the target of kidnapping in Iraq."

"I've taken my precautions, Colonel. Previously, during the coronavirus epidemic, as a representative of the CDC, I was once taken hostage by Chinese villagers in exchange for medicines. I've been wearing various microtransmitters in the heels of my shoes ever since. The signal can be detected up to nine miles away by radio receivers or by a GSM network. Thanks to a connection with the GPS–satellite network, a microtransmitter's location can be pinpointed exactly. That means I can be traced, should I ever get abducted again. I'll provide you with the radio receivers."

The next day, Shira left in a Humvee, with Kadeem and the military escort, for Samawah. They reached the city after half an hour's drive down the freeway along the River Euphrates. It was a typical Arab city, with light-brown blocks of houses, crisscrossed with broad avenues, and dominated by various mosques. It had been constructed on both sides of the Euphrates and was surrounded by hundreds of palm trees providing some welcome shade from Iraq's searing heat. The people of Samawah had a number of simple and inexpensive ways of brightening up their city: murals on the gray concrete walls around official buildings and schools depicted lifelike, everyday scenes.

The oldest section of the city was a maze of bustling markets and streets. They eventually arrived at the modern Sadiq al-Ahli hospital in downtown Samawah, where they parked. Once inside, they met Farrah al-Rashid, who was recovering from an illness. Shira spoke with Farrah through Kadeem, who acted as an Iraqi Arabic-English interpreter.

"Hello, Farrah; my name is Shira Fox. I'm a scientist."

"Hello, Miss Fox; what do I have to thank for your visit?"

"I'd like to ask you something about the ancient city of Uruk."

"What do you wish to know?"

"I saw various crevices in the ground in Uruk. Could you please tell me some more about those?"

"Indeed I can, Miss Fox. These are there so that at night, straw-colored fruit bats come to eat dates from the date-palm plantations around the village of al-Khidhir. At sunrise, they vanish into the crevices in the ground to refuge beneath the earth."

"I'd like to visit those refuges sometime," Shira remarked.

"Beware!" Farrah warned. "Satan and his evil spirits dwell there! Whoever dares to follow the fruit bats never returns again!"

Farrah's story made Shira realize that the excavation team needed a speleologist for investigating the caverns. Caving expert Charles Cappart, aged thirty-four, was tracked down. He was eager to take part from the outset. Charles was flown over from France to reinforce the excavation team. Shira was there waiting for him at the camp's heliport.

"Hello, Charles, I'm Shira Fox, the expedition's epidemiologist. How was your journey here?"

"Excellent, Shira. I'm happy to be able to support the team with expertise."

"I see you've brought more than just your expertise along."

"That's right. This equipment is for exploring caves: overalls, helmets, head torches, harnesses, lifelines, grips, ropes, whistles, waterproof containers, artificial lighting, and even gas masks."

He took a gas mask out of the box and put it on. "See? How do I look?" he asked.

"Like Darth Vader," Shira remarked.

"Shira, I am your father. Give yourself to the dark side," he said in a deep voice.

"Ha-ha, nice, but let's have no more jokes about my father.

He died young. That taught me independence early on, and that's why I'm here right now, potentially saving the world."

"*Mon Dieu!* My apologies, Shira."

"Don't worry, I'm thick-skinned But first we still have to find that cure in the demonic caves under the temple in Uruk."

"And that's where I really come in. You can count on me. The devil doesn't scare me!"

"That's great to hear, Charles!"

"What do you actually mean by demonic caves?" he asked.

"If we're to believe the clay tablets, we'll be exploring the hellfire of Ereshkigal, goddess of the Sumerian underworld. Everyone feared her. That was more than five thousand years ago. These days, the local population believes Satan lives there."

"Great company! Those prospects sound really attractive! When do we start?"

"As soon as the excavation team has unearthed the gates underground. They're currently surveying the ground under the temple with soil-penetrating radar. That way, they can map out the subterranean structures."

"No technology spared on this expedition," he said.

"There's a great deal at play, Charles. Humanity's future is at stake. We simply can't cut any corners. That's why we've also brought you in."

"You can be sure, I won't let you down. Caves are my favorite habitat. That's to say … as an enormous hobby. I'm an IT instructor by profession because you can't make a living from just caving."

"Speaking of IT, that actually reminds me that I'm going to mention you in my blog this evening—that is, at least, if you don't have any objection. This blog is read by millions of people around the world who want to follow the expedition's progress. We're actually on our way to becoming the internet's latest stars."

"No problem, Shira. I'll provide you my brief curriculum vitae, so you can add firsthand information to your blog."

"Thank you, Charles. I appreciate that!"

Shira thought that Charles was a friendly and helpful guy. They got on well right away.

⁂

Meanwhile, Barbro wasn't sitting idle. She would sometimes keep company with the German archaeologist Odo Holz. Both had very little on their hands at this phase of the expedition, and that gave them plenty of time to chat.

"I see you're reading a book, Odo?"

"Yes, *The Art of War* by Sun Tzu, a Chinese general who lived around 500 BC, in the Warring States period."

"I know that book!" Barbro answered. "That man established a system of rules for each phase of military conflict. It's a standard work on warfare and strategy, and nowadays it's still used by strategists, generals, and even managers since those rules appear to work in any environment where there's competition, such as competitiveness between companies, marketing, politics, and sport."

"That's right," Odo said. "His recommendations focus a lot more on alternatives to conflict, such as cunning, delay, using espionage, and alternatives to war itself, forging and retaining alliances, using deceit, and the readiness to subject oneself, at least temporarily, to more powerful enemies. There are numerous famous quotes from the book: "Know the other and yourself, and victory will not be at risk! The best military strategy is attacking the enemy's plans—then comes preventing hostile alliances; then the assault on the enemy army, and the worst is attacking a walled city."

"Appear weak if you're strong and strong if you're weak. All warfare is based on deception. This is why, when we are poised to attack, we do not appear poised to do so; when we use our force, we must appear inactive. If we are in the vicinity, we must have the enemy believe that we are far away. When we are far away, we must have him believe we are in the vicinity," Barbro added.

"Have your plans be as dark and impenetrable as the night

and, when making your move, come down like a thunderbolt," Odo said.

"Build your opponent a golden bridge for him to retreat. Do not take on an enemy who is more powerful than you. And if it is unavoidable and you must engage, ensure that you enter into this on your own terms, not on the terms of your enemy," Barbro concluded.

"The expert in conflict moves the enemy and is not moved by him. The ultimate art of war is to subdue the enemy without fighting. He who wishes to fight first, counts the costs," Odo retorted.

"Ha-ha, we could go on forever!" Barbro noted. "I see we're evenly matched."

Barbro and Odo discovered that they were both sly-minded, and they started appreciating each other more and more.

The radar-team leader shared his findings during the daily briefing on how the expedition's activities were progressing. "As hoped, the earth-penetrating radar has revealed various subterranean structures under the temple and in the vicinity of the temple. On these photos, you'll see there must be some kind of passageway connecting each cavity together."

"It's not all that clear," Shira noted.

"That's down to large sections of the passageway being filled in, I guess with sand or rubble—meaning the radar image is less sharp."

"Okay, that's plausible," Shira said.

"In any case, we now know where the passageway starts under the temple, and the excavation team can concentrate on that area."

"That's excellent news. I'll have the excavators get started on that spot tomorrow. Thanks for your explanation!" Shira said.

One day, Odo decided he wanted to win Barbro over. To make an impression, he confided in her a theory he'd devised concerning the Great Sphinx of Egypt. "The Great Sphinx on the Giza Plateau, hewn from massive rocks, is Egypt's most important sculptural work, and nobody knows with certainly who had it carved and why. It's a mystery. The current supposition is that the Great Sphinx was hewn under Pharaoh Chefren of the Fourth Dynasty. The reason for this is that the Pyramid of Chefren is located behind the Great Sphinx, when approached from modern Cairo. However, the Great Sphinx has certain stylistic features, such as the folds under the headdress. These are among the first examples of headdresses, particularly a fragment from the head of the Cheops statue, which, nowadays, is kept in the Metropolitan Museum. This suggests that the Great Sphinx was carved under the Pharaoh Cheops. Cheops is the father of Chefren."

"Cheops had the Great Pyramid built, didn't he?" noted Barbro. "It's one of the Seven Wonders of the World."

"That's true. Cheops has a penchant for colossal construction works. Another element can be found in Cheops's face. On the only statue of Cheops we know of, the lower section of the face juts out, just like with the Great Sphinx. This condition is known as prognathism. This could perhaps also explain the Egyptian name of Cheops, namely Khnum-Khufwy, which as far as we know means protected by the god Khnum. The god Khnum was depicted with a ram's head displaying a similarity to prognathism."

"What a find," said Barbro.

"That's not all. Listen to this: The Great Sphinx ought to be viewed in profile, like the Egyptian depiction of an animal, human, or god, or like an Egyptian hieroglyph representing an animal or human. In this case, it's not the Pyramid of Chefren but the Great Pyramid of Cheops that's behind the Great Sphinx, just as if you were approaching the Giza Plateau from Memphis, the ancient Egyptian capital."

"Bravo once again," Barbro applauded.

"And finally, the icing on the cake," Odo said, triumphant.

"The head of the Great Sphinx is too small compared to its body. This indicates that the Great Sphinx must have originally been built with a different head, which was later resculpted into the human head we're familiar with. What head would it have been originally?"

"I wouldn't know. Maybe a lion's head, matching with the lion's body?" Barbro suggested. "The lion is a sun animal, and the Great Sphinx is looking due East, where the sun rises."

"That could be so," said Odo. "During the Fourth Dynasty, the Pharaoh was associated with the cult of Ra, the sun deity. Graham Hancock and Robert Bauval, authors of the pseudoscientific book *The Message of the Sphinx*, claim that the Great Sphinx initially had a lion's head, and this even dates from 10500 BC, because at that time, it looked toward the constellation Leo, the lion, during the spring equinox sunrise. Nevertheless, this theory can't be right, because the constellations of the zodiac originate from Mesopotamia and were entirely unknown in Egypt until the much-later Greco-Roman period."

"You've got a point there!"

"However, I've got another idea. The ancient Egyptians saw the language of the gods in the landscape. You already know the name of Cheops means protected by the god Khnum. If you then view the Great Pyramid, Cheops's final resting place, standing behind the Great Sphinx—protected by the Great Sphinx, as it were—a suitable head for the Great Sphinx in that case is the head of the god Khnum, so … a ram's head! The landscape then pronounces the name of the pharaoh, like in a rebus, protected by the god Khnum."

"Whoa!" Barbro exclaimed, "what a fantastic discovery!"

"And there's more. The pharaoh is responsible for divine order on Earth. The Great Sphinx with a ram's head and a lion's body stands for Khnum-Ra. Khnum is the god responsible for the annual flooding of the Nile with its fertile sludge, and Ra is the god responsible for the daily rising of the sun. The Great Sphinx with a ram's head symbolizes divine order on Earth, or the pharaoh himself."

"That all sounds entirely plausible!"

"A large hole is located in the head of the Great Sphinx," Odo continued. "This might have been used for attaching a ram's horns."

"Can you also explain why the head was changed into a human head?" Barbro asked.

"There's a stele recounting that the Great Sphinx was struck by lightning. The lightning knocked off a section of the head. I therefore assume that the head was damaged to such a degree that the only option was to create a different and smaller head. In that case, a depiction of the pharaoh's head would have been chosen."

"You really are so inventive, Odo!" Barbro gushed. "I love creative people who venture to think outside the established box. Can your theory ever be proven?"

"I'm afraid not. There are hardly any texts dating from the time of Cheops and Chefren, in the Fourth Dynasty. Herodotus, who visited Egypt in the fourth century BC, reports that there were strange symbols on the capstones of the Great Pyramid. In AD 1179, the Arab historian Abd el Latif wrote that the inscriptions were so numerous that they would fill thousands of pages. William of Baldensal, a European visitor of the fourteenth century, recounts how the stones were covered with strange symbols arranged into careful rows."

"They must have been hieroglyphs!" Barbro noted.

"Indeed. An earthquake occurred in 1356, after which the Arabs unfortunately removed the capstones in order to rebuild mosques and forts in Cairo. The stones were recapped in smaller pieces. This meant that all traces of the ancient inscriptions that could have told us who had the Great Sphinx built and why disappeared."

"And so you're left with your wonderful theory that you unfortunately can't publish for lack of evidence. To console you, I'm inviting you to my tent this evening. There you'll learn all about my divine order …"

The sun went down, but the evening was still warm. Odo had taken a shower, put on pants, no shirt, and approached Barbro's tent. "Hey, Barbro, can I come in?"

"Come in, Odo!"

She was wearing an enticing red skirt that accentuated her feminine curves to full effect, despite the dim lighting. He gave her a kiss that she responded to with her sensuous mouth.

"Sit down, Odo. Can I offer you something to drink? I have Coke and Schweppes tonic."

"In that case, a tonic, to quench my thirst."

She gave him the drink, went to stand behind him, and started massaging his shoulders.

Odo closed his eyes and savored the moment. When he opened them again, she was standing next to him. He looked at her, and she straddled his lap, her eyes full of longing. She placed both of her hands on his shoulders. She then let her hands slide down and stroked his bare chest.

"Barbro, I'm finding it hard to resist …"

"So just let go, honey. That's what I want."

Barbro snuggled up closer to him, until he felt her breasts pressing against his chest. She blew into his right ear and nibbled it gently.

"Now, let me be here for you," Barbro whispered. She pressed her lips against his. He let her do as she pleased. She won him over by caressing her body against his most sensitive part, and he surrendered.

With his hands under her buttocks, he stood up from the chair. She had wrapped her legs around his waist, and he made his way to the more comfortable bed. He dropped her onto it and stood still for a moment, gazing at her.

Barbro laughed seductively and bit her lip. She took his hand and pulled him toward her. He joined her on the bed and took her in his arms. His fingers felt the zipper on the back of her skirt, and he opened it. He then carefully lowered her shoulder straps. She wasn't wearing a bra. He started to stroke her breasts and erect nipples.

"You've got a great body, Barbro."

She giggled, unzipped his pants, slid her hand into the opening, and touched his crotch.

"Show me what you've got, bad boy."

Odo spent a night of passion with Barbro. She was certainly gifted when it came to lovemaking. Odo proved himself to be an ardent lover. After that night, he was entirely under her spell. From then on, he called her *Isis-Hathor*, the Egyptian goddess queen who had many associations, such as beauty, joy, power, maternity, healing, and destruction.

Barbro deemed the time ripe for taking Odo into her trust concerning her intentions. "Odo, honey, I've thought of a plan that will make us mega rich."

"Oh, really? I'm listening," said Odo.

"This is it. When we find the cure, I'd like to steal it and sell it to Farmoso to give them a monopoly in manufacturing and selling the medicine. There are a billion people infected in the world. Farmoso will be able to earn so much with the medicine, that it'll want to pay me handsomely to provide it with an effective, working remedy. I'm talking millions of dollars, depending on the medicine's research and production yet to be determined."

"An enticing amount, but how do you plan on stealing the cure from Alexander and Shira? They don't seem like such pushovers."

"Just leave that to me," she said. "The most important thing is that, as Alexander's backup, you can translate the Sumerian clay tablets, and you're able to find out the cure."

"And how do you imagine evading the coalition? They won't be happy about your plan one bit. Without help from coalition troops, we'll never get out of Uruk. We're stuck here. How can we have the cure's effectiveness tested and negotiate the final sale to Farmoso?"

"I've already worked this out. The closest Farmoso site to here is in Turkey. Transportation from Uruk to Turkey runs largely over roads in Iraq that are unsafe, in view of the country's unstable political situation. That's why we're working with an anti-American faction in Iraq, the Jaish al-Mahdi. I've found them and have already contacted them through the faction's English-language website for recruiting jihadi fighters worldwide. Jaish al-Mahdi group members will see to transporting us to Turkey, in exchange for receiving the first medicines produced."

"If we do that, we'll fall out of favor with both the coalition and the home front, Barbro. I can forget all about my life in Germany, but what about your life in the United States and your job at Harvard?"

"I'm prepared to burn my bridges and to make a new life for myself outside the United States, thanks to the profits I hope to gain out of this. What do you think, honey? Are you ready to follow me?"

"I'd go to hell for you, Isis-Hathor. I'm ready to follow you, wherever you go. We're a couple."

CHAPTER 7

The excavation team discovered the first gate in Sumerian style under the House of Inanna and Ereshkigal in Uruk. It then proceeded to remove mounds of earth and rubble, thus clearing the tunnel. One obstacle they encountered was a deep pitfall containing the skeletons of previous grave robbers. The team then went on to find the following gates, one by one. Each one was adorned with a depiction of the goddess Inanna, relinquishing an item of clothing, as in the Sumerian myth of her descent into the underworld.

A US television team had arrived to film the excavation's progress. Shira and Alexander spoke with them in an interview.

"Shira, why is this expedition so important? Why so much expense and effort?" asked the reporter.

"We have strong indications that the cure for the current epidemic is written down on clay tablets located under the temple of Inanna and Ereshkigal in Uruk," Shira answered. "Once we find those tablets, we can greatly reduce the search for a medicine, which would otherwise take years and would be extremely expensive. We can't let any opportunity slip by. That's the reason for this expedition."

"How far has the excavation got?"

"The tablets are located behind the seventh gate under the temple. The excavators are currently busy exposing the fifth gate. That means we've made good progress."

"How can we read those clay tablets?"

"They're written in Sumerian cuneiform," Alexander

answered. "They're more than five thousand years old. Together, with my colleague Odo, I'll see to translating these."

"Following this, our colleague Barbro will provide the pharmacological interpretation," Shira continued. "I will examine this translation from an epidemiological angle. We're forming a multidisciplinary team on site to react as swiftly as possible."

Among those in the United States viewing the broadcast of the report were Sarah and Ralph. They once again sensed a glimmer of hope.

Later, Shira saw news reports stating that certain countries in the Middle East that had not been so severely affected by the epidemic, such as Iran, Yemen, and Syria, were issuing a ban on people and animals traveling from the United States, Europe, and the Far East. Elections had been held in Iraq. Power was shifting from the Coalition of the Constitutional State to Iraq's Islamic High Council, a party closely allied with Iran. Iraq was threatening to cease its support for the coalition. This meant that if the excavation team still wanted to achieve its goal, it had to double its efforts.

At that moment, Shira was visited by the head excavator. "Shira, bad news. The digger's broken down."

"Can it be repaired?"

"No. We've tried, but we don't have the right spare parts. We'd better have a new digger brought over, then."

"Damn it! That's really not good right now, when it's more urgent. We have to demand that new machine immediately. I'll ask Colonel Mackay to arrange transporting it."

While waiting for the new machinery, Shira sought a way to relieve the tension that was consuming her. She knew that in cases like these, classical music could help. She grabbed the flute she'd brought with her in her luggage and went with it to the ruins of

Uruk, which were now quiet and abandoned, and played Bach's Sicilienne.

Charles was drawn by the sound and savored listening to the music in these odd surroundings. When Shira was done with playing, he applauded enthusiastically.

"Wonderful, Shira! I never knew you played an instrument! A hidden talent!"

"Yep, that flute's an heirloom from my father. I'm really fond of it. Playing it makes me calm."

"That's so cool!"

"I love that music. The composers I like listening to most are Brahms, Saint-Saëns, and Tchaikovsky."

"Really? They happen to be some of my favorites too. Their best works are on my smartphone. If you want, we can go and listen to them."

"That's really kind of you, Charles! See you soon, then?"

An hour later, Shira and Charles were sitting and enjoying the music he was playing through speakers in the computer room. Shira wanted to write her blog in the evening as usual, but computer issues arose. Fortunately, Charles was still close by. He solved the problem thanks to his expertise as an IT instructor.

"Okay, Shira. You can get to work now!"

"Charles, you're an angel!"

She gave him a kiss in gratitude. However, it was more than gratitude. She felt tremendous affection developing for this man. From the way he looked at her lovingly, she could tell he must also be feeling attraction.

A new digging machine was flown over to Uruk the next day, meaning the excavators could resume work. Shortly afterward, Alexander went to Shira in a frenzied state.

"Shira, it's unprecedented!" he exclaimed.

"What's the matter?" asked Shira.

"Words fail me. The sixth gate has been damaged by the excavators. In their haste, they failed to handle the digging equipment with due care. The relief of the goddess Inanna has been irreparably destroyed."

"Well, I'd asked them to hurry up with excavating the tunnel. It's a shame about that relief, but you just can't make an omelet without cracking some eggs."

"And now you're justifying it. That's horrendous. Ancient images ought to be preserved!"

Barbro was drawn toward Alexander's rumpus. "What's up, Alexander?"

"Barbro, the relief on the sixth gate has been wrecked by the rabble of clumsy excavators—and before I was even able to take any photos of it."

"Oh, if that's it, I can put your mind at rest. I was exploring the tunnel yesterday evening and took photos of that with my cell phone. Although they're not the most professional, they're better than nothing. Here, take a look."

"Barbro, you're my ministering angel! This means the gate in its original state is still preserved in photographic form. Thank you, darling!"

"My pleasure, Professor. If I can be of any further assistance, just let me know! I'm also really good at massages …"

"Well, in that case, you can practice your arts on my weary limbs this evening in my tent."

"You can count on it," said Barbro, stroking his beard.

"Barbro, without you I couldn't bear it in this dusty hole. Thank you for being there."

Shira had gotten wise to Barbro's seductive side and remarked, "Barbro, after Odo, you're now also wrapping the professor around you finger?"

"Mind your own business, Shira. You're hitting it off with Charles, aren't you? Shouldn't you be with him?"

The professor added a retort. "That's right, Shira, you

wrecker. Go off to Charles and allow us, culture-loving people, to do our work."

Shira felt personally attacked but also realized she had to defuse the situation. "Professor, I understand that you're angry. The situation is tense after the damage to that relief. That wasn't intentional. I'll see to it that this never happens again and will instruct the excavators to be careful so the cultural treasures can be spared."

"That's something, at least," said Alexander. "But I do not want to hear any more comments about Barbro."

"I understand that you require relaxation," Shira admitted. "There's nothing wrong with that. Just remember what the purpose of this expedition is. We're here to uncover and translate the clay tablets to find a medicine. All the rest is peripheral and could distract us. I expect everyone to stick to his or her role and duties. Is that clear?"

"Loud and clear, general!" answered Alexander.

"Most definitely!" Barbro concurred.

A large cave was found between the sixth and the seventh gates, where the fruit bats roosted. The ground was strewn with mushrooms, which thrived in the bats' dung. Shira could curb her curiosity no longer and she made sure she was the first at seventh gate, without waiting for the speleologist, Charles Cappart. Upon her arrival, she encountered a man with a tunic and a long beard.

"I am Neti, the guardian," said the man. "Who are you?"

"I'm Shira."

"What led you to set your heart on the path from which no traveler returns?"

"I have come to find the parts of the Mes that are found in the underworld."

"Please remove your jewels and garments before I might allow you to pass!" Neti requested.

Shira obeyed, walked through the gate, and found herself face-to-face with a winged, female demon: Ereshkigal.

"A mortal in the underworld!" Ereshkigal cried. "Cursed be! The Anunnaki, the judges of the underworld, shall pass judgment over you!"

Grotesque creatures with birds' heads encircled Shira.

"Because you have dared to enter here, we sentence you to death so that you would remain here for eternity."

A feeling of dread consumed Shira. She attempted to flee and turn back to the seventh gate. However, Ereshkigal was too swift for her and impeded her way.

Shira plowed into Ereskigal with all her might to force her way through. This came down to a fierce grapple between them. For a while, it was uncertain who would gain the upper hand. Shira fought for her life, yet Ereshkigal possessed supernatural powers. Exhausted, Shira was simply no match in this uneven struggle against the demon. Shira fell to the ground and lay there, dying …

Shira awoke in the camp's sickbay. She saw Charles standing by her bed.

"Charles, what happened? How did I get here?"

"Do you remember? You were in the cave, and you went to the seventh gate?" Charles asked.

"Yes, I remember that."

"From the sixth gate, I saw you fighting against some invisible opponent at the seventh gate," said Charles. "At the same time, I saw the mushrooms you'd crushed when you walked over to the seventh gate. From my caving experience, I understood that this is a species of mushroom the spores of which, if inhaled, have a hallucinatory effect. I rushed out of the cave right away and went to the excavation camp to fetch the gas masks I'd brought with me from France. After that, I took some of the excavators with me, wearing gas masks, back to the cave with the mushrooms.

You were lying on the ground, unconscious. We carried you to the camp and gave you oxygen to neutralize the effect of the hallucinogenic spores. A short while later, you woke up."

"I sure had a horrible nightmare. My head's still throbbing. I'm lucky you could save me, Charles."

"You can say that again. You gave us a real fright. Had you been in the cave an hour longer, those hallucinogenic spores would have killed you."

"I owe you my life. Thank you, Charles!"

Charles' concern for her charmed Shira. She gave him a long, deep embrace. A romantic connection between them rose. Nevertheless, the urgent situation they were in stopped them from giving their burgeoning feelings much attention.

Later that day, Shira, Charles, and Alexander entered the cave wearing gas masks.

"Just be careful," Charles warned. "We might have gas masks on, but we'd better step on the mushrooms as little as possible so we don't corrupt the air in the cave."

"Here's a way around the mushroom field," Shira noted.

"That must previously have been used by the temple's high priests to reach the seventh gate," Alexander suggested.

They followed the detour to the seventh gate.

"The seventh gate is decorated with the image of a man with a tunic and a long beard," said Shira.

"That's Neti, the guardian," said Alexander.

They passed through the gate and arrived at another large space carved out from the rock. Their torches cast beams of light and ghostly shadows on the walls. They could make out winged figures. Some of them had birds' heads.

"Here are different Sumerian statues," Charles noted calmly.

"Those are Ereshkigal and her judges, the Anunnaki," said Alexander.

"I saw the image of Neti and these statues as real beings during my hallucination," Shira imagined.

They penetrated further into the darkness. There, they found various alcoves hewn into the rock with decorated wooden boxes.

"These are presumably the graves of kings or high priests," Alexander remarked.

Lastly, they discovered various recesses in the rock, in which they found dozens of stone plates.

"Hurray!" cried Alexander. "Here are the clay tablets! We're almost there!"

That evening, Barbro made her way to Alexander's to massage him as agreed.

"Hey, Professor. It's Barbro."

"Hi, Barbro. Come in. You can just call me Alexander."

"Are you all set for a relaxing massage, Alexander?"

"I most certainly am. Grab the bull by the horns! Allow me to disrobe and lay down on the bed."

Once Alexander was settled on the bed, Barbro set to work. "Your hands work wonders. It feels marvelous," he told her.

"I heard you made a major discovery at the seventh gate," she said.

"That's right! We found the clay tablets. Several have already been brought to the surface and are in the tent with the archaeological objects. Tomorrow we'll start scanning them in and translating, using the equipment I brought along."

"That's so exciting!"

"It truly is. I can hardly wait to get started. But for now, I'm enjoying this massage. You're an expert."

Once the massage ended, and after the day's commotion, Alexander nodded off. While he slept, Barbro squeezed a couple of drops of the laxative Laxoberon into his personal hip flask of whiskey.

The following day, Alexander was displaying symptoms of diarrhea. It was assumed to be stomach flu or stomach typhoid. He was flown over to the helicopter deck ship for medical treatment. He would spend a few days there, since he couldn't resist nipping a drink of the whiskey in his flask, fully unaware that drinking this was causing his predicament.

In the meantime, Odo saw to translating the clay tablets himself. Besides inventories of sacrifices, the tablets also included the section of the Mes stating the remedy against the infertility epidemic. Once Odo had read and translated that text, he could barely contain his excitement. He notified Barbro immediately, without informing Shira.

"Barbro, I've found it!"

"Not so loud, Odo. What did you find?"

"The cure! It involves eating the stalks of the mushrooms growing in the cave between the sixth and the seventh gate!"

"Hmmm, fantastic." Barbro guessed, based on her pharmaceutical expertise, that the mushroom stalks would appear to contain antigens that, once consumed, stimulate the body's immune system to produce antibodies against the Human Fertilodeficiency Virus, thus curing it.

"I assume you'll require a few samples of the mushrooms to be able to produce the remedy?" he asked her.

"That's right. We'll have to try getting ahold of them tonight, Odo! Then we can take them to the Farmoso site in Turkey. Based on the spores, Farmoso can cultivate entire mushroom fields."

"How do we get out of Uruk once we've got the mushrooms?"

"I'll notify my Jaish al-Mahdi contact person in advance to send someone by jeep to pick us up at midnight at the main entrance to Uruk. That jeep will have to drive through the desert to circumvent the military camp, but that'll be no problem."

"Excellent! Our secret has a chance of succeeding. So I'll now go back to my office with the clay tablets and pretend I'm translating."

"Remember to pack the clay tablets with the cure on them, Odo. They're coming with us."

"Hey, Odo," said Shira when she came to visit him later on.

"Hey, Shira."

"How's the translation going? You found anything yet?"

"I'm still translating away. Up to now, it's only been about sacrifice inventories. But I'm not losing hope. Maybe I'll find the remedy on the tablets I haven't translated yet," he said. Then he changed the subject. "How's Alexander doing?"

"Not so good, Odo. He still hasn't recovered. He won't be back anytime soon. That means all hope for the translation is with you."

"I'm doing my best. I know a lot depends on this."

That night, Shira was unable to sleep. She had the feeling that Odo was concealing something from her. She went for a final stroll before going to sleep. Suddenly, she made out two dark figures, with torches and gas masks, heading toward the temple. They vanished into the passageway to the gates. Shira quickly thought about what to do, and then went to Charles's tent.

"Charles! Charles, wake up!"

"Huh, what? Oh,Shira, I was just dreaming about you."

"Sure you were, charmer!"

"Why are you waking me? What's the matter?"

"I saw two people entering the passageway with the gates. It's eleven o'clock!"

Charles stretched himself. "That definitely isn't normal. Let's go take a look."

Charles quickly got dressed, and together they sneaked to the temple. Everything was quiet. There was no longer any trace of the figures to be seen.

"Maybe they're a pair of antiquity looters," Charles suggested. "We should keep an eye on the entrance, waiting until they come out again. Then we can give them the third degree."

They waited until they saw two figures come outside. It was Barbro and Odo, carrying a box. They were startled when Charles and Shira suddenly appeared in front of them.

"Barbro, Odo, what are you doing at night in the seven gates? And what's in that box?" Shira asked.

"We're trying to verify something Odo found on the clay tablets," Barbro answered evasively.

"*Nom de Dieu,* you're trying to steal our remedy, aren't you? Give us that box!" Charles demanded.

"I'm afraid we can't do that," Barbro responded. "But we'd appreciate it if you allowed us to leave with the box. I'm offering you each fifty thousand dollars in exchange for your silence."

"No way," answered Shira. "We can't be bribed!"

"Shira's totally right," Charles confirmed. "For the last time, give us that box!"

Barbro suddenly drew a weapon and shot Charles. He fell to the ground.

"Charles!" Shira cried. She knelt down by his body as her eyes welled up with tears. "We have to get help!"

In response, Barbro threatened, "If I were you, I'd just keep your trap shut, Shira. You're coming with us as a hostage. Try not to resist. Otherwise, I won't hesitate to shoot."

With Charles left for dead, Shira followed Barbro and Odo. *What a monster,* Shira thought, *and I invited her to join the expedition. How could I have been so blind to Barbro's intentions?*

Barbro and Odo walked to the main entrance of Uruk, with Shira as a hostage, and took the jeep that was waiting for them. They drove to Samawah, the city eighteen miles to the west of Uruk. There they met with other members of the Jaish al-Mahdi faction, who were planning to take them on to Turkey.

The shot Barbro fired hadn't gone unnoticed in the camp, and things were in an uproar. Charles was found, wounded but alive, and taken to the sickbay. He was visited by Colonel Mackay.

"Hey, Charles," the colonel said. "What happened?"

"Oh, Colonel, it was Barbro and Odo! They stole the remedy, shot me, and took Shira as a hostage."

"Any idea where they're headed?"

"I heard an automobile start and drive away, but I don't know where."

Colonel Mackay immediately ordered a large-scale search for the fugitives. The helicopter-deck ship went into action. All escape routes were blocked by coalition military personnel. From the air, American aircraft and helicopters scoured for the getaway car.

Colonel Mackay then recalled the microtransmitters in Shira's heels and had investigative teams seek out the signal with radio receivers.

Barbro, Odo, and Shira left Samawah with cars from the Jaish al-Mahdi faction. Unnoticed, Shira managed to leave behind some transmitters along the escape route during stopovers. That allowed the investigative teams to follow their route from Samawah to Rumaythah, al-Hamzah to Diwaniyah, and al-Hashimiyah to Hillah. The path went in a northwestern direction.

Eventually, the two cars were apprehended because of a coalition-troop roadblock between Hillah and Bagdad.

Sitting in the first car were the Jaish al-Mahdi driver, Barbro, Odo, and Shira, who was handcuffed. The coalition troops shot out the car's tires.

It dawned on Barbro that she was trapped and that she had to act quick. She leaped out of the car and ran, disregarding the bullets, to the second car, where there was space for one more. She took that space. The second car then performed a full U-turn, evading the blockade.

The first car fell into the hands of the coalition troops. Odo was taken into custody, and Shira was freed. Shira interrogated

Odo. "Odo, the game's up. If you cooperate, I might be able to do something for you. What's in that box?"

"Some mushrooms," he admitted. "Those growing in the cave between the sixth and the seventh gate."

"Why? Have they got something to do with the cure we're looking for?"

"Yes. Eating the stalks provides the cure, according to the clay tablets we took. Barbro thinks they contain antigens."

"Oh, that's valuable information! Where is that clay tablet?"

"Still packed in the car."

Shira took the package with the clay tablet and had it transported by a V-22 Osprey tiltrotor aircraft to the camp. Once she and the tablet arrived, she placed it in a safe in the tent with archaeological objects. She then visited Charles in the sickbay.

"Hey, Charles. I'm so glad you're still alive!" she said.

"Shira, what a relief you managed to get away from those gangsters Barbro and Odo!"

"Yep, the adventure is all over. The coalition troops freed me. Odo has been arrested. Barbro managed to get away, but I have the clay tablet with the remedy. How are you?"

"On the mend. Thank God Barbro's bullet didn't hit any vital organs. Otherwise, I'd be a goner."

Shira hugged Charles carefully and kissed him.

"You know something? You had me worried sick there," she let slip.

"Same here. My thoughts were always with you. I was praying you'd get out of this alive."

"Charles, you're a sweetheart."

The cause of Alexander's "illness" was also discovered. He recovered and returned to the excavation camp where he met with Shira.

"Shira, I'm so happy to see you again! I heard about what

you went through. Barbro is such a bitch. She took us for fools. Luckily, it turned out well!"

"You can say that again! It was certainly touch and go at one point. I have the tablet we were looking for. Can you please verify its translation?"

"I'll do that right away!"

A short while later, Alexander returned with his translation, elated.

"Shira, the cure involves eating the stalks of the mushrooms!"

"So Odo was right. Wonderful! I'm putting my plan into action!"

Shira provided the remedy and a few samples of the mushrooms to pharmaceutical companies the world over. They, in turn, cultivated the mushrooms in larger quantities. From these, they succeeded in extracting the antigen, and even synthesizing it. This opened way to mass producing the medicines, which then had to be tested on humans and approved by national governmental bodies, such as the Food and Drug Administration (FDA) in the United States. Sarah and Ralph, who were among the very first victims of the epidemic, volunteered as trial subjects for the tests.

As usual, three phases with increasingly larger human clinical trials were conducted. The initial phase investigated toxicity in general with healthy volunteers. The second phase comprised studying the body's influence on the drug and vice versa, and the dosages with patients. The third stage was a large-scale investigation into the effectiveness among the patient population in question. These tests were successfully concluded. The FDA evaluated all the data and was able to accept a positive risk-benefit assessment. The products were approved for release into the United States market. Other countries followed suit.

Pharmaceutical companies produced the medicines in large quantities, and governments distributed these among the infected people at fair prices. To determine who should be given the medicines first, in each country, the initial letters of each first name were drawn by lots, until every letter was dealt with.

In the world's conflict zones, military assistance was required for distributing and administering the medicines.

EPILOGUE

The global population had been saved. People were once again able to travel and have face-to face contact. The internet restrictions were lifted, to the immense joy of those advocating freedom to browse.

Sarah was also cured. Not long after, she became pregnant. She was over the moon. The pregnancy thrived without a hitch, and the child's room was furnished just how she wanted it.

Odo was convicted of stealing extremely valuable information and heritage. His sentence was five years in prison. Barbo was convicted in absentia for attempted murder, theft of extremely valuable information and heritage, and abduction. Her sentence was life imprisonment. Based on the Patriot Act, Gary Olson was convicted of terrorism by intentionally spreading a hazardous biological substance, and he was jailed for twenty-five years.

Alexander took great care of the clay tablets they found, reassumed his position as professor of ancient languages at the University of Pennsylvania, and swore never to touch whiskey again.

Following his recovery, Charles relocated to Atlanta in the United States to be closer to Shira. He found a job as an instructor, and they started living together. They were finally able to enjoy each other's company in peace, and they made a happy couple. In his free time, Charles explored the caves in the state of Georgia.

One day, Sarah was watching the news.

"Ralph, come see. There's a clip about our heroes on CNN!"

"Yeah? Let's watch!"

The commentator gave the following introduction: "Epidemiologist Shira Fox and caving expert Charles Cappart were received in the White House today. The president wished to thank and reward them personally for their part in combating the past epidemic."

The president said: "Ms. Shira Fox and Mr. Charles Cappart, thanks to your courage, ingenuity, and perseverance, we were able to beat the global infertility epidemic. I hereby bestow upon you the Presidential Medal of Freedom, the highest American civil distinction, for your especially meritorious contribution to a significant public undertaking."

"Really well deserved," noted Ralph.

"Sure is," Sarah agreed. "Without them, I'd never be expecting now!"

After nine months, Sarah and Ralph were able to call themselves the proud and ecstatic parents of their first child. The bundle of joy weighed nearly eight pounds, and was already a strapping 19.2 inches tall.

Once they were back home from the hospital with the baby, their neighbor Olivia was, as ever, sitting on a chair on her veranda, observing. "Sarah, Ralph, congratulations on your baby!"

"Thank you, Olivia!" answered Sarah.

"Is it a boy or a girl?"

"She's a girl!"

"That reminds me of my own daughter, long ago. What are you going to call her?"

"Shira, like the scientist who beat the epidemic."

"Well, okay … It's hardly original, but it's a great tribute!

The world needs strong women to get the better of the wolves in the world."

"Strong women with empathy, that's for sure!" Ralph concurred, winking at Sarah.

And thus came to an end what historians would go on to call the Great Infection.

Thank you.

Back in 2003, I took the course called Screenplay Writing at the Flemish Script Academy, with the intention of one day writing a story for a film or comic. For some time, I had been brooding on a tale involving the Sumerian myths of Inanna's Descent to the Underworld.

I wrote the first synopsis in 2012. After positive feedback, I went on to elaborate this into a fully-fledged novel.

I would wish to thank all my family, friends, acquaintances, and colleagues who have supported me in this.

AUTHOR BIOGRAPHY

Carl T. Seaborn was born in Belgium in 1964 and studied at the University of Ghent for civil engineer physics and electronics. He has a passion for culture, history, and science. He has always been fascinated by art in all its facets. He draws, paints, photographs, makes logos, and writes stories and articles.

Ereshkigal's Vengeance is his first novel. He wrote the book between 2012 and 2020, anticipating the coronavirus pandemic of 2020.

Printed in the United States
by Baker & Taylor Publisher Services